Brian Aldiss, OBE, is a fiction and science fiction writer, poet, playwright, critic, memoirist and artist. He was born in Norfolk in 1925. After leaving the army, Aldiss worked as a bookseller, which provided the setting for his first book, *The Brightfount Diaries* (1955). His first published science fiction work was the story 'Criminal Record', which appeared in *Science Fantasy* in 1954. Since then he has written nearly 100 books and over 300 short stories, many of which are being reissued as part of The Brian Aldiss Collection.

Several of Aldiss' books have been adapted for the cinema; his story 'Supertoys Last All Summer Long' was adapted and released as the film *AI* in 2001. Besides his own writing, Brian has edited numerous anthologies of science fiction and fantasy stories, as well as the magazine *SF Horizons*.

Aldiss is a vice-president of the international H. G. Wells Society and in 2000 was given the Damon Knight Memorial Grand Master Award by the Science Fiction Writers of America. Aldiss was awarded the OBE for services to literature in 2005.

The Bright █ Diaries

BRIAN ALDISS

The Brightfount Diaries

The Friday Project
An imprint of HarperCollins
77-85 Fulham Palace Road
Hammersmith, London W6 8JB

www.harpercollins.co.uk

First published in Great Britain in 1955 by Faber and Faber Limited
This edition published by The Friday Project in 2013

Text copyright © Brian Aldiss 1955

Brian Aldiss asserts the moral right to be identified as
the author of this work.

ISBN: 978-0-00-748210-8

Typeset in Minion by
Palimpsest Book Production Ltd, Falkirk, Stirlingshire

For my dear 'Polly'

You are the music while the music lasts

About half of this material originally appeared in the pages of *The Bookseller*. For permission to reproduce it here – and for many other kindnesses – I am indebted to the Editor, Mr Edmond Segrave.

Introduction

This is my pet book – the book with which I first dipped my toes into the chilly waters of publication.

Some time after WW2 was over, I returned from the East seeking the grant I would need in order to attend university. I was eventually told that the ex-service grant system was closed.

So, I took an ill-paid job in an Oxford bookshop. At least I was to be among books, those friendly fruits.

The official magazine of the book trade was, and still is, *The Bookseller*. Weekly copies were circulated among the staff. In the fifties, articles were published about the 'big cheeses' who comprised the book trade. There was no mention of those slaves, like me, who actually manned the counters and faced the customers.

I wrote a letter about this state of affairs to the editor of *The Bookseller*, a Mr Edmond Segrave, saying that 'the pale face of the bookseller's assistant was the backbone of English literature.'

Mr Segrave enjoyed the joke and dropped me a line in return. It was then that I conceived the idea for a series of comic sketches set in an imaginary bookshop.

Mr Segrave summoned me to his office. I wore a tie for the occasion. He said they had never published, never tried to publish, a comic series. If I would write six of these proposed pieces, he would consider them to see if he found them funny.

So, that I did. I worked near the celebrated Oxford bookseller, 'Blackwell'. So, playing on this, I chose the name for my fictitious shop: Brightfount's.

Those weekly instalments began to appear in *The Bookseller*. Publishers, it was reported, were amused.

'Brightfount's' had been appearing regularly for about two years when I received a letter from Mr Charles Monteith of Faber and Faber. He asked if I would care to turn my weekly column into a book.

During the next six months, six other publishers wrote to me with similar proposals. But I could not have had a better publisher than Faber, nor had a more pleasant man to deal with than Monteith. He and I had two items in common; both of us as boys had subscribed to *Modern Boy*, (which published original 'Biggles' stories), and both of us had served in Burma, fighting Japanese forces.

I have always been confident. But about two weeks before *The Brightfount Diaries*' publication day, I suffered the equivalent of stage fright. The public! – What if they don't laugh?

Fortunately, they did. My long shambles of a career had begun.

Brian Aldiss
Oxford, 2012

June

Last week at 'Hatchways'. Shall be sorry to leave here, partly for Aunt Anne's sake – she is becoming afraid of being left with Uncle Leo – and partly because I shall miss the country. Shall even miss that seven mile cycle in to work each morning, which I have cursed so often.

Been glorious day. Just looked out of my window to see, low over Claw Marsh, sun setting behind Drabthorpe Priory, while down on the lawn Uncle Leo stood knee deep in the fish pond.

'Whatever are you doing there?' I called in some alarm.

'I hope I have not warped the course of your life too much,' he bellowed back. 'You must remember I have had to sacrifice a lot for your mother; she has been a difficult woman, Derek, a difficult woman – always remember that.'

'This is Peter up here,' I called back, not without embarrassment, remembering Colonel Howells next door was probably within earshot. 'What are you doing?'

He climbed slowly out of the water, shouting as he did so, 'I'm just considering erecting some tessellation instead of that parapet; it would just break the line of the roof nicely. Come down here and see.'

'Not if it means standing in the middle of the fish pond.'

1

Nevertheless went down. Uncle was standing there wringing out his trousers. Asked him cautiously what made him call me Derek.

'Got the boy on my mind, you know, with him coming back to England soon,' he explained. 'Shouldn't be turning you out otherwise.' Then he rapidly changed subject and said, 'You work in a bookshop. Bring me back any books on tessellation you have.'

Can't remember single book on tessellation at Brightfount's, but Uncle must be humoured. My cousin Derek and his wife Myra and her sister Sheila are all descending on Uncle and Aunt, to live at 'Hatchways' until they can find house of their own. No doubt prospect makes him feel a little odd.

MONDAY

Borrowed Huxley's *Doors of Perception* for the weekend. He advocates a substitution of the drug mescalin for those dubious Western narcotics, cigarettes and alcohol. Was carried away by his fervour (Huxley always mesmerises me). Eager to experience the beatific vision, I hurried round to Loghead and Beale, the chemist's, in the tea break, and ordered a half gramme of mescalin.

'Mescalin?' the chemist asked, puzzlement in his voice.

He knows me well, and at first I thought he was merely surprised to find I was not after aspirins. But it transpired that he had never heard of mescalin. Nor did he find it in the pharmacopoeia.

'Huxley experimented in California,' I said.

'Ah . . . That explains it. It's American.'

So have not experienced that blessed state of beatitude; instead, feel merely a slight frustration. The only consolation about the business is that I described Huxley's book so glowingly to my chemist friend that he parted with six shillings for a copy on the spot!

Publishers show a business-like alacrity to link books with films: would not a similar arrangement with Boots be easy to make? How fascinating to organize a 'Read the Book – Taste the Drug' campaign.

Or perhaps a limited edition could be produced complete with an unbreakable phial of mescalin contained in a back flap. Such a reasonable policy might bring considerable financial rewards; for instance, the tome would probably be chosen as the Underworld's Book of the Month.

TUESDAY

Travellers much in evidence. What nice hats the Heinemann men wear!

In the quaint, gangling structure known as the book trade, the publishers' travellers play an important part. Like bees going from hive to flower they provide vital links between the strongholds of London W. and such shabby outposts of literacy as Brightfount's.

Had to barge into Mr Brightfount's office while M—'s rep. was there to get a book set aside for someone. Mr B., looking very cheerful, hands in pockets, canting his chair back dangerously, was saying, 'Of course you know *we* never had any *Ascent of Everest* on subscription order!'

Thought this quaint thing to boast about, later realized it must have been a counter-gambit to a new mountaineering book produced as 'another Sir John Hunt'.

Sold our second-hand copy of Augustus Hare's *Walks in London*. Noted from its costing that it was bought into stock year I was born. Twenty-five years on one shelf! Hope it gets a good home.

Pretty busy in afternoon, but found time to play one of Mrs Callow's hard little games. Think she organized it to brighten up old Gudgeon, who wears far-away look: it gets further away as his holidays get nearer.

Object of this game was to think up literary animals. Thurber had a peke called Darien: did we know any other such pleasant beasts? Dave announced that a Maori had a little lamb, but this was disqualified. We could only produce that hybrid, the old English Bear-wulf, and a Gorbuduck. So Mrs Callow won with a Shakespearian nursery animal called Fardels Bear.

At this point Mr Brightfount appeared, and we returned to our posts. The bear presumably went back to Hoo Wood.

Actually found a book on fortification in our Architecture for Uncle Leo. We are a bit short of staff at present, have been since Miss Harpe departed, and on top of that Edith was away to-day with a

3

cold or something. So I left shop late, and cycled slowly home enjoying sunshine. Arrived at 'Hatchways' to find Uncle had gone to bed.

'What's wrong with him?' I asked Aunt.

'Nothing, as far as I can make out. He simply said he wanted to go to bed with the birds.'

'But the birds won't be going to bed for two or three hours yet!'

'You remember those stuffed owls and things in glass cases up in the front attic? He's gone to bed with them. I don't pretend I'm not worried.'

WEDNESDAY

Our junior partner, Arch Rexine, and I spent most of the morning cataloguing. Trade very quiet. A traveller in to see Mr Brightfount, reappeared to tell us the one about the Army Captain and the frog who turned into a beautiful princess in the middle of the night.

Just before closing, about ten to one, a flock of people came in, talked volubly together without looking at the shelves and left after a quarter of an hour without buying anything.

Dave hastily put the blind up, but before he had turned the key one of the talkative group thrust his head in again and said, 'I say, I forgot to ask – have you a copy of *Local Government and Local Expenditure*?'

'Our books are under alphabetical order of authors,' Dave said sourly. 'Who's it by?'

'Oh. I forget. I had it written down but I've lost the piece of paper.' With that he retreated, and Dave locked the door.

'You know who that lot was?' Mr B. said, emerging from his office with his hat on. 'They've come down for the local conference. They're Efficiency Experts . . .'

Half-day. Beautiful sunshine. Helen and I swam in the river down past Poll's Meadow. Not a soul about.

Where do people go to in the summer countryside? Except for Helen and me, everyone might have been sucked up with the morning's dew into heaven. We soaked in water and sun, and I felt perfectly content – *pro tem*, anyhow – to remain on earth.

THURSDAY

Foreigner, a Belgian, in shop in morning asking for Galsworthy's Saga. I tried to imply that Kingsley Amis' *Lucky Jim* presents a more up-to-date, if narrower, picture of us.

'It must be Galsworthy,' he said. 'It is for my friend at home who has never heard of Galsworthy.'

The answer still puzzles me – not so much its meaning as its implication: one of us, despite all appearance to the contrary, was not understanding the other perfectly. What then will his friend make of Soames? (Somewhere here is hidden a pointer to international co-operation.)

Later, while I was wrapping the parcel, I asked our visitor how he liked England (stupid question!). He said he did like it, that it was his first visit here, and that he had always wanted to come over because 'several of my parents were born in England'.

(Somewhere here is hidden a pointer to international co-operation.)

FRIDAY

A. H. Markham, an old customer and a bit eccentric, bustled in as we opened after lunch and went straight to History. He seized on our new copy of Tate's *Parish Chest* (C.U.P., 25s.) and stayed there with it till we closed. Now and again he would pop a peppermint in his mouth and make a note on an old envelope.

Commented Mrs Callow as we trooped out to get our bikes: 'Quite a tête-à-Tate.'

More cataloguing in afternoon.

SATURDAY

Probably most authors realize how profitable it is to be published in America. Came on an old advert to-day that proclaimed Hammond Innes as the Englishman with most serials in the *Saturday Evening Post* to his credit. That'll make some of his rivals wistful! Not that wistfulness will help them get into the *Post*: the demand is evidently for forthright action.

Still, as Lionel Johnson remarked a while ago:

Some players upon plaintive strings
Publish their wistfulness abroad.

Moral: There may not be a market for every book, but there is for every mood.

Apropos of which, when Dave complained to Mr B. once about some ancient stock, he got the surly answer: 'There's a customer for every book, young man.'

'The trouble is,' Dave said later, 'half of 'em are dead.'

Nice to get out of the shop into the summer air. Just getting on my bike when Mr Mordicant appeared; I did my Army service with his son. He is something on the local *Journal and Advertiser* but never seems to do any work. Ribbed him about this; he said, 'Well, I'm making a kind of social survey. Nothing organized, you know, but I like watching the odd fish that swim around the tank of post-war England.'

'Suppose it's not much different from pre-war?' I hazard, not quite knowing what to say.

'Quite different,' he said. 'Everything's changed. People have got an entirely new attitude. You'll see – I'll write a book about it some day.'

He's certainly right about odd fish.

June–July

Moving day for me. Surprising what lot of junk I've managed to accumulate in three and half years here. It's been home from home indeed, real home being eighty miles away and too far and expensive to get to every week-end. In afternoon, Uncle drove down with me to new digs, which certainly will be handy for the shop.

Landlady is one Vera Yell, nothing much to shout about. Think even Mordicant would agree she is definitely of pre-war vintage. Her husband was once Uncle's auctioneer. House is one of row of six. My room is up two flights of stairs, looks out over feeble gardens, outhouses, tumbledown walls, backs of other houses and cathedral behind them all.

Room itself is typical bed-sitter; an effort to make it habitable has obviously been made, so don't grumble. Mrs Yell showed it to me very defensively. 'I'm afraid the furniture's not especially new,' she said.

'As long as it's comfortable . . .' I replied, glancing rather apprehensively at large photo of large girl in gym tunic hanging by the door.

'Oh, that's my younger sister Grace,' says Mrs Yell hurriedly. 'I hope you wasn't expecting Picassos.'

'Of course not.'

'What with them and atom bombs and the Russians, and

now these poor plastic children, I don't know what the world's coming to.'

'Oh it could be worse.'

'Yes – and probably will be before it's better. Anyway, I'll bring your breakfast up prompt at eight each morning.'

MONDAY

Breakfast was prompt: cornflakes and cold sausage. Walked round to Brightfount's.

Spent most of morning doing window. Made glorious mêlée of new, second-hand and remainders on theme of 'Diaries and Diarists'. Am always afraid of getting price tickets wrong since the time we marked a set of Hakluyt £8 8s. instead of £18 18s. Our nice morocco Pepys as centrepiece; it's been in before, but no matter.

Cross Street looked very pleasant in the sun.

Mr B. spent most of day pricing the library he bought from Professor Carter. One volume had been a gift from a famous author and bore the inscription on the fly-leaf: 'To D. C., A Parting Shot.' The book was *A Bullet in the Ballet*. Was this only the mild joke it seemed, or a veiled but straight tip to D. C. to stay away? An association or a dissociation copy?

TUESDAY

Slipped out in morning to buy new pair of white flannels, passed two young men talking so animatedly and with such pleasure that I was attracted to them straight away. As they whisked by me, I only caught three words, uttered by one of them in excited tones: '*I*'ve been reading . . .' Pass, friend.

V. nice flannels. Expensive. Wore them to tennis with Helen in the evening. Had about enough of her. For one thing, her service is putrid.

WEDNESDAY

Very busy; generally are on half-day. Gudgeon, our senior assistant, had the day off, so most of serving devolved on me. Still no replacement for Miss Harpe, who left in the spring because she was asthmatic and allergic to dust.

In the middle of a rush, some thoughtless millionaire came in and bought our morocco Pepys from the window. Very awkward: nothing decent to fill the gap.

According to Dave, who always ferrets out such tit-bits of information, Mr Brightfount interviewed young girl who starts Saturday; know Mr B.'s choice by now: plump, greasy, prone to sniffing. We've got one like that on the staff already – poor old Edith, dumb office wench.

Irritable. On bike ride, Helen and I caught in heavy rain shower. Violent quarrel under horse-chestnut. That's over! Returned to digs and was furiously barked at by Mr Yell's dog in the hall. Retreated to room: 'Lost myself in a book.'

Relevant quote from *Rasselas*: '. . . the incommodities of a single life are, in a great measure, necessary and certain, but those of a conjugal state accidental and avoidable.' Must see about getting married; am old enough, if not rich enough. Trouble is, there are few suitable girls – only the Dodd girl, whom I don't know very well, and Colonel Howell's daughter Julie, who works in London. Shall probably end up bachelor like Gudgeon; a lifetime of Mrs Yell's breakfasts stretches before me.

THURSDAY

Gudgeon bought a portfolio of prints for ten shillings yesterday and sold it to Mr B. for two pounds ten. Said he to me, waving the spoils, 'There's a beautiful bit of engraving on these notes, you know.'

He starts his holiday on Monday.

Saw Helen in Cross Street. Grrrr!

FRIDAY

Pay-day. Packet seemed thinner than ever. 'Here's to the next one!' old Mr Parsons says each week as he tucks his envelope away.

Arch Rexine loathes to throw a book away; Mr Brightfount pitches them out with heart-warming prodigality. I've had several interesting volumes from our 'chuck-out pile'. Have just found old novel called *Store of Gold*. Pubd. in the twenties, it is a tale of a future where Big Business has run wild; goodness knows, it may have been credible when it was written. Now, it is alternately funny and fustian. Hero and heroine work in a giant store which stays open twenty-four hours a day, seven days a week. Employees work four hours on, eight off, sleep in gigantic dormitories miles underground. Hero, transferred to Toys, is separated from heroine; book details their struggle to meet in lifts ('non-stop express to all seventy floors') and wangle a reunion. It's comedy-Kafka – or perhaps burlesque-Bennett.

My favourite character was Menucius Replay, who works in the book department. To Menucius ('the constant burning giant gas jets had etched an ineradicable pallor in his gaunt face') is given the soul-destroying task of writing two-hundred-word reviews for the weekly publicity sheet of all 'failed books' and books cut in price; that is, remainders.

We are told one day, 'the conveyor deposited before Menucius his quota of work for the next two shifts: a two-volume autobiography of an obscure statesman, a biography of Hannibal, *Days Afloat, More Days Afloat*, three novels with a religious bias, a symposium on modern science and a book of egg recipes. After but a second's hesitation, Menucius reached out for Hannibal. Life's desperate struggle for survival had taught him already to tackle the toughest while he was freshest.'

Dipped into this treasure while dusting and sorting Foreign Lit.

Mrs Callow, just going into Rexine's room to take his letters, was slightly nonplussed because a customer asked her for *Airs of Old Venice*. She looked in Music, couldn't find it, and told the customer so. Gudgeon, without a word, fished the book out of Foreign Hist.: *Heirs of Old Venice*.

Explaining later, Mrs Callow added, 'I never turned a heir.'

Which reminds me. Had a hair-cut to-day. Looked at an old *Men Only* while I waited my turn. One cartoon showed an impressive boss saying to applicant for job: 'We want reliable men here,

11

self-confident, strong-willed men, capable of saying to their wives, "No dear, I will *not* ask for a rise".'

To tennis club in evening. Played one game singles with ginger, freckled chap from Midland Bank.

SATURDAY
Would you believe it!

The rumoured new girl has arrived! And very nice too . . . Slender, nice high forehead, hair the colour of grapefruit squash. Name: Miss Ellis. She'll be working in shop with me. Brightfount's is looking up!

Helen just *asked* for this.

Chap came in during afternoon trying to sell Rexine glass shelves and chromium stands. Rexine, surveying with dignity our ancient, scarred wood, said, 'My dear man, we can't flout tradition; there's been a bookshop on this site since 1820.' The dear man suggested it was time for a change.

'You don't know the book trade,' Rexine said, retreating from his dignity with a laugh. When the traveller had gone he added contemptuously to me, 'Glass shelves! With you and Eastwode beefing about!'

New girl confided before we shut shop that she's 'terribly fond of symphonies'. Told her I'd just bought Bizet's No. 1. Good start.

On strength of this, roughed out sentimental little article on book-selling that I may offer to local paper. It ends with this telling (?) summary of the job: 'The trade that pays so little and gives so much.'

July

Rather overcast in morning, but cycled dutifully over to Graves St Giles to see Uncle and Aunt. House in chaos, owing to the grand turn-out in honour of cousin Derek and his bride, who return from Singapore next Friday week. Doubt if Aunt will ever have the place ready in time.

Slightly insulted to see how thoroughly they have thought it necessary to clean my room. It was stripped of everything bar wallpaper.

Uncle Leo paced up and down it excitedly, gesticulating as he did so. 'I wouldn't have any furniture in the house at all, if I had my way,' he says, adding in lower key, 'not, as you know, that there is ever any likelihood of my having my way here.' I know nothing of the sort, Aunt Anne being the gentlest of women, and he continues hastily, 'My whole life's been devoted to selling empty houses, as was dear old Pa's before me, and believe me, they're vastly better without being cluttered by a miscellaneous welter of furniture. You don't smother the outside with lumber – why spoil the inside?'

Now he is warming to his theme. In trying to sell an odd idea to me, he – how often have I seen him do it! – sells it to himself. A house should be a shell, filled only with the spirit of its inhabitants, a sort of homely monastery. He has forgotten about the necessity for beds, chairs, tables . . . If he had his life over again, and was free of the tedious necessity of running a miserable, moribund little estate agency (a job he loves), he would live indoors and cultivate his soul. 'As it is, my soul's all whiskers and bottom.' He'd take up Yoga, a sort of Westernized Yoga.

'Lunch is ready, dear!' Aunt calls.

'The voice of authority,' says Uncle. 'Come on, may as well eat. Don't know what Derek and Myra will think of this room – it's the draughtiest in the house.'

Mr and Mrs Yell are very kindly couple. Would insist when I got back that I went into their living-room and had a slice of cold pork for supper with them.

MONDAY

Workmen in, doing new shelving job in cellar. Ever since I've been here there seem to have been workmen romping round.

Poor old Mr Parsons, who as our packer looks on the cellar as his own domain, much put out by this strange activity round him.

'Trouble with them', he tells Rexine, 'is they talks too much. Their boss is a bloke called Vaws; I reckon it ought to have been Jaws, because that's all he does, jaw, jaw, jaw!'

Spent long while sorting out order for University of Lehukker in America. Dave, seeing me begin to dust a thickly coated set of Lytton, cries in mock-horror, 'Don't do that! Our only chance of getting rid of a bit of dust is to send it away with the books!'

Few customers about. Was sent after lunch-hour to get on with 'Slaughterhouse'. This derelict bit of shop is crammed on all sides with unsorted volumes, piled on the shelves in no order. Being on ground floor, it is all too convenient place to store second-hand books when they are bought to await pricing and categorizing later. But in bookshops, later never comes. There always seems too much to do.

Amusing to note people's attitudes to the Slaughterhouse. Miss Harpe, who left in the spring, always referred to it as 'the Miscellany Room' and refused to go in it. When customers find their way in, they either exhibit extreme displeasure to find such disorder or extreme delight at such a gallimaufry.

Gudgeon, our senior assistant, is on holiday. He spends all his holidays with equally silent friend, fishing up and down England. Poured with rain most of day; let's hope the fish are rising well.

TUESDAY

Our new assistant, Miss Ellis, is not turning out quite as well as (I) expected. For her looks, much can be forgiven her, but was much shaken to hear her pronounce 'Goethe' as 'Go-Ethe', the second syllable to rhyme with 'sheath'. Unfortunately, Mrs Callow, in whom the vein of satire runs deep, also heard it. Suspecting my leaning for Miss Ellis, she devised, and repeated throughout the day, this chant:

> Goethe, Goethe,
> What very prominent teeth!
> They make you look a swine
> Compared with Heine, with Heine.

Mr Brightfount in reminiscent mood. While Arch Rexine made himself ostentatiously busy, Dave, Mrs Callow and I listened with interest. It does not sound much fun to me to have earned only a guinea a week, but everyone who has tried it seems to have enjoyed it – in retrospect, anyway.

Mr B. started in the approved fashion, the hard way. 'I've gone without many a meal to buy myself a volume I coveted,' he admitted with a shade of pride. He is quite right, of course; one of my favourite memories of myself is sitting empty in pocket and stomach, reading Clive Bell's *Civilization*. It would not have excited me half as much over fish and chips.

Mr B. says, 'I explored every avenue connected with books,' a nice metaphor that gives him a country background. But it was in London that he bought a partnership in a small publishing house. They are still functioning, and have just published *By Bicycle Up Everest*.

Dave asked him why he had thrown that venture up and returned to bookselling.

He chuckled. 'Publishing?' he said. 'There's no money in it!'

At closing, Miss Ellis was met by offensive young fellow who took her arm and led her possessively away.

WEDNESDAY

Very neat van stopped outside Fletcher's, the nearby café. Little windows in either side showed bright books. Sneaked out to have closer look. It was an Oxford University Press children's book van. Asked the driver where he was going. He winked and said, 'Cambridge.'

Half-day. Tennis: not playing well this year. Polishing up my little article on bookselling, wrote it out neatly as possible, and posted it to the *Journal and Advertiser*. Don't suppose they'll have it. If they do take it and pay me for it, I shall buy myself a new pair of white socks.

THURSDAY

Life is very irritating really; nothing turns out as planned. Meant to get up early and go for walk but overslept. And Mrs Yell had burnt the toast – not for the first time, either. Mrs Callow greeted me with her nasty chant:

> *Goethe, Goethe,*
> *What very prominent teeth.*

But the afternoon was lovely. Mr B. and Rexine both had to go out, and Mrs Callow was upstairs helping Edith, our dumb office wench.

Dave and I chatted with Peggy – Miss Ellis. Sun shone, warping boards of escape books' display in side window. Doors open: a dandelion seed drifted aimlessly in. Sold two expensive prints.

Cross Street seemed to dream in the sun. In the church next door, someone was playing the organ superbly. With the sound and the sun and the books and Miss Ellis, life suddenly achieved a pattern, rich and satisfying – and how old the pattern was, though the organ pipes were but recently installed and the books fresh from their authors' hearts.

Or are books written mainly from the head?

Anyhow a feeling of tranquillity permeated the air. As we lolled on the counter, Dave recounted his most exciting moment in a bookshop. The war was on, and he was alone in shop with a nervous evacuee woman who came to work afternoons only, name of Flossy. The time for closing was drawing near; there were no customers within miles.

It was a soaking wet November night; out of the blackout came a wild-looking giant who commenced to prowl up and down the shelves. He wore no raincoat and his suit was saturated, but he paid no heed, merely dashing water out of his hair. Totally ignoring the two behind the counter, he marched round the shop like a being demented.

Flossy was alarmed. Did Dave think he had *escaped* from anywhere? Dave said nonsense; but the big man was certainly behaving queerly, leaping from section to section, pulling out a book here and a book there. Some he crammed back on the shelves, some – almost without glancing at them – he formed into a pile on the floor.

'See what sort of stuff he's going to buy,' Flossy hissed; she was all for phoning the Home Guard. When the odd man's back was turned, Dave sneaked over and glanced at the top book which had been selected. Its title made his hair stand on end: *The Criminal Responsibility of Lunatics.*

He had just informed Flossy of this when there was a power failure. All the lights went out. Dave was nonplussed, but not Flossy; she started to scream. Fortunately, the electricity reappeared in a minute. The stranger was gone.

Miss Ellis, who had been listening raptly, breathed, 'Had he stolen any books?'

'Of course not,' Dave said. 'That dream Flossy must have terrified him. He ran out in a panic!'

Postcards arrived from Gudgeon, who spends his precious fortnights fishing in Norfolk. He sent me one this year for the first time – makes me feel quite important member of staff! Mr B. and Rexine got sober views of Lowestoft, Dave and I got broad behinds and red noses.

Gudgeon being away, Dave has to do the *Clique*, a duty conferred on him by Mr B. as if it was an honour. Perhaps it is, but this is difficult to determine from Dave's demeanour.

The *Clique* is one of the insts. of the book trade. Every week, at a thousand bookshops scattered over the British Isles, people pop in and ask for books which are not in stock. Not only are they not in stock, they are frequently out of print, often are completely unheard of, and are entirely fictitious. The only method of obtaining these phantoms is to advertise for them in the *Clique*. To the non-bookselling eye, *Clique* has little to attract: it contains over a hundred pages blackly printed in double columns. These two hundred odd columns consist of authors and titles required by the scattered and hopeful booksellers. This means some nineteen thousand common or scarce books in all, and all ordered! There is a fortune waiting for anyone who could supply them all. But in a week's issue we rarely report more than a dozen titles, and rarely get answers to all our requests.

All the jokes in *Clique* (and there are few) are accidents, and not very funny. To see someone advertising for Henry James: *The Golden Bowel*, is amusing only after thirty pages of dull and correctly printed titles.

Saturday
Work.

Poor old Peggy does very well for a beginner really: but today Edith discovered she has been entering everything up wrong in the day-book. Rexine amazingly patient – if Dave or I had done anything like that we should have been hanging by now from the sign over the entrance.

Sunday
Over to Graves St Giles. House in slightly better order.

Uncle very quiet during lunch, vanished afterwards without

drinking his coffee. Aunt Anne looked very depressed, so asked her when we were washing up if I could do anything.

She shook her head and said, 'He's getting so *eccentric*.'

'Is it because Derek and Myra are coming home next week?'

'No – only indirectly.'

She looked as if she might have said something else, but at that moment I happened to let go of a plate, which changed the subject. Before taking her usual rest, she had a sherry, a bad sign.

Went for rather aimless walk hoping perhaps I might see Julie Howells, returned to find Uncle still away and Aunt in orchard, slashing vaguely at some nettles with a sickle. She looked up and began speaking before I could so much as greet her.

'There's something I ought to tell you, Peter,' she said. 'I think you ought to know, although we've always kept it even from your mother and father. Come and sit in the loggia.'

Obeyed, thoroughly alarmed.

'You know D. H. Lawrence had scores of collaborators?' she began.

'Yes,' I said, not committing self.

'Well, he had anyway.' Long silence. 'You know your uncle is a literary character?'

'I know he's known Mr Brightfount a long time.'

'My dear boy, your uncle used to be a reviewer.'

Said I had not heard this before.

'I am afraid your mother and father have never been very booky people . . . However, that's nothing against them. Mr Brightfount has never told you anything of this?'

Forced to ask Of What?

'That your uncle once collaborated with D. H. Lawrence?'

At last the bomb was dropped! Of course was wildly excited by news, although furious to think of years wasted without knowing of this. What would Mrs Callow say when I told her?

'Sit down and don't behave so childishly . . .'

Begged her to tell me all about it, how it had happened, what they had written.

'It was early in 1922,' Aunt said, 'and your uncle reviewed *Aaron's Rod* in the local paper — it used to run a literary column once a fortnight until the old editor died. About a week later, Lawrence appeared at Newspaper House and asked to see your uncle.'

'How marvellous! Had Uncle given it a good review?'

'Far from it. We were living in the little house at Lower Wickham then. Lawrence arrived in time for tea.'

Seemed to me to be most wonderful thing I had ever listened to! Asked if they fought like dogs.

'Not at all. He stayed eleven days. I did not care for him – we had only been married a little while – your uncle and I, that is. You could hardly tell at times that he was in the house – Lawrence, I mean.'

Asked what they wrote.

'Oh, nothing that was ever *published*, of course. They were working on an idea that was going to be called 'The Gypsy and the Virgin Kangaroo', but it all fell through, and afterwards Lawrence made two other books out of it.'

Asked why on earth Uncle and Aunt had been so quiet about all this.

'Well, it was not long after that Lawrence published *Lady Chatterley's Lover*, and your uncle had always been well thought of locally, so . . .'

Uncle appeared at that instant through the side gate, bearing in his arms an enormous bundle of bulrushes, so that I never heard what effect Lawrence's visit had upon his eccentricity.

Write this all carefully down now not just because it is the only important thing which has ever happened in our family, but because it is valuable scrap of history in its own right. Can't think why Uncle did not write book on Lawrence; lots of other people did.

MONDAY

Wasted twenty minutes over one customer – and sold her nothing. She wanted a good English grammar that would do for her two boys for reference at home. I felt I knew those wretched children personally before she left: Dennis, aged nine, Wilfred, fourteen. 'We want to give them really good careers. Trouble is, we can only afford it for one of them. Ought we to concentrate on Wilfred, who's the elder? – but he's always been so slow – or cut our losses and just plug for Dennis, who's frightfully bright for his age?' Etc., etc.

Finished with the suspicion that she wanted neither book nor advice, just a chat about her troubles. Odd how people unburden to strangers!

Can't help worrying about Wilfred, though. If he doesn't watch it, he'll end up as a bookseller's assistant.

Tennis in evening: singles with the Dodd girl. Bought her a squash afterwards. May see more of her.

TUESDAY

Late. Rexine saw me come in at 9.15, just looked. Expect I'll hear about it some time.

Been thinking about yesterday's customer. Her problem is much the same as a bookseller's; to push the old, slow stock or concentrate on flogging what is already doing well? In Brightfount's we've never decided.

Mrs Callow's birthday. Gave her a box of chocolates – only person on staff who gave her anything. Dave and I invited up to her house this evening, went by bus. Very nice there. Food first class. Mr Callow science-fiction enthusiast, to Dave's delight – we went for walk, left them chatting and diving excitedly into vast cupboard full of magazines with bright, neat astronomical covers and titles like 'Stupendous', 'Staggering' and 'Unlikely'.

Have not said anything to anyone about Lawrence. Rather wish now I was going out to 'Hatchways' next Sunday, but have already planned to go home for week-end.

WEDNESDAY

Half-day. Rained. Bored. Should not be reading Kafka's Diaries if they weren't remaindered. Very good bargain.

Few customers show much interest in anything to do with books apart from whatever particular one they are after – except when it comes to remainders. Name seems to waken their interest. 'Why are they so cheap? How can you afford to sell them at this price? Do the authors know about this?'

Any number of answers really. Most of our reduced books are not our own dud stock, but come from firms who buy up from publishers. Publishers get rid of books for several reasons, most of which they do not mention, for remaindering is not the glorious business publishing is; all publishers remainder, none do it with cocktail parties. Pity, that!

You are cordially invited to

A COCKTAIL PARTY

at

The Algernon Hotel, Bifold Street,

on

the – July, 19—,

in celebration of the clearance of the last seven hundred and seventy-three copies of Mr ABLE-FURBISH's *Still More Writing Really at Random* for one shilling and twopence apiece.

TIES.   R.S.V.P.

And this because, perhaps, the publishers have overprinted a good book, to be on the safe side and avoid reprinting later. Or perhaps they had overestimated the market for that particular book (already glutted by Mr Furbish's previous works, *Writing Really at Random* and *More Writing Really at Random*). Or perhaps Mr Furbish wanted a holiday in Old Calabria and required a lump sum in a hurry. Or perhaps his book had been rather drably produced. Or perhaps the publisher's production manager had cut his costs on the book jacket, and nobody liked the look of the thing at all.

Or perhaps – which is quite likely – it was just a rotten book.

THURSDAY
Up v. early in burst of energy for swim by Poll's Meadow. Back pleased with self and peckish. Landlady, spotting me, commented irritably,

'Fancy getting yourself hungry like that before breakfast!' (She operates under fixed impression rationing is still on.)

She was annoyed again at tea when I came in filthy from the shop. We moved two old sets of Scott from the Slaughterhouse to the basement and I had cobwebs on shirt and hair. Mrs Yell: 'Now just look at you! And I thought books was a gentlemanly profession.'

'Not the retail end,' I explained wearily.

We all had some of Mrs Callow's birthday cake in tea-break. Peggy Ellis promised to bake some buns and bring, one day. Dave, being funny, said he would bring some beer. Peggy: 'You won't really, would you?' (She is disappointingly naïve)

Dave: 'Of course I would. Why, last Christmas I brought some wine and we got old Brightfount so pickled he couldn't say "Hodder and Stoughton".'

I heard him telling her later that this Christmas we would have some mistletoe. Those two are getting very friendly, suspect romance in the air; but offensive young fellow still meets Peggy outside shop about twice a week.

Workmen have finished in basement, Vaws has gone. Old Mr B. looking very miserable all morning; perhaps he has had the bill. He spent long while shut in office with Rexine. We know these moods of old. Everyone apprehensive; the next devel. is generally a lecture by Mr B. on saving electricity, paper, etc., commencing with the words, 'I've just been looking at the figures . . .'

'He's probably seen the announcement that U.K. booksellers had a turnover of forty-four million pounds last year,' Dave said, 'and thinks he's not getting his fair cut of it.'

Sudden inrush of customers then, including A. H. Markham who wanted back a book he sold to us two years ago.

We still had it.

FRIDAY
Pay-day.

Tucking her envelope away, Mrs Callow observed, 'Well, we must be grateful for small purses.'

Had my article on book-trade back this morning: 'not of sufficient general interest'. Bang goes another promising literary career.

Expected lecture materialized to-day, before we went down to cellar for morning tea. Gathering us all together in the back of the shop by Rexine's office, Mr B. commenced, 'You'll be interested to know I've just been looking at the figures . . .' Usual talk followed. Try and save string.

The man from the public library came in shortly after and ordered a lot of Biggles books, which seemed to restore humour all round. He and Mr B. get on well together: they were Fire Watchers or something in the war.

Royal Family books selling well – especially on Fridays, market day. Farmhouses hereabouts must be full of them.

Customers not exciting on the whole. We have one or two people whose visits we look forward to: Owen Owen, the town councillor, Ralph Mortlake, who is rather an ass, Prebendary Courtnay, rather stiff, Professor Carter, vague, and of course A. H. Markham, who distributes sweets. And there's old Maclaren, whose appearance we dread. And the plump fellow we call our Thief, although we've never actually caught him taking anything.

Of course, there is also Jocelyn Birdwine, but he hardly ever comes in nowadays. He was the most odd and charming person you could imagine. Now he owes us £4 14s. 6d. and has ceased to call.

Sometimes people make their inquiries so disinterestedly, so tediously, looking away or yawning as they do so, that I long to scare them back into showing a semblance of intelligence. What a luxury to wait until they've fumbled into silence and then to drop the dummy mask of assistant – saying in the most freezingly rude tone, 'Now get back outside that door, come in briskly and say your piece coherently, and then we'll see what we can do for you.'

Had a lovely customer in before we closed, fully compensating for a hundred stodges. She was dark, slender and sad, but smiled most beautifully. Imagine her name was something Shakespearian, probably Miranda. A car waited outside for her – I saw her climb into it with a flash of graceful legs, watched it move down Cross Street. Alas, she must be bird of passage; she bought an Ordnance Survey map of country south of here and then was gone.

> *Books of poets dead and gone*
> *What Elysium have ye known—*
> *This one day, in Brightfount's tavern,*
> *A spirit lit your spirit's cavern!*

Met Miss Dodd (Avril) with her brother after work. Spent agreeable evening with them. Returning late down Cross Street, saw lights on in Brightfount's; could make out poor old Mr B. up in his office. He works so hard. Who'd be a bookseller?

SATURDAY
Gudgeon's last day of holiday!

The people you know best are not your friends but those you work with: Arch Rexine, for instance, our junior partner. He was serving an imposing-looking man this afternoon who wanted Shaw first editions. The mere mention of Shaw and Rexine's homely face lit up.

'I don't know if you've ever heard this Shaw story,' he began modestly. He goes on to describe how Shaw sent one of his plays to a famous but penurious poet, whom we will call S.Q. The play was inscribed, 'To S.Q., with affection'.

But S.Q. was hard up, took the play to Charing Cross and sold it profitably. There, browsing a day or two later, G.B.S. happened to discover it, no doubt with relish. Next day, S.Q. received the play back through the post; under the previous inscription was written, 'With renewed affection, G.B.S.'.

Rexine trots this tale out regularly. Any mention of Shaw, S.Q., or association copies and out comes the story. If you said 'G.B.S.' to him in his sleep, he would reel it off. But it is a good story. Must tell it myself when Rexine's not about.

Got the 6.50 train home, tra la!

SUNDAY

Luxurious to wake between decent sheets. Did not realize till now that Mrs Yell's smell of mothballs and toast.

Brother Andrew has delish. new waistcoat. His photographic business seems to be doing well from all appearances. Says airily to me, 'In a couple of years I may be able to take you on as a junior.'

'What'll you pay me? Enough to buy pansy waistcoats with?'

'Not likely – but by then I may let you wear this one.'

Think I'd rather stay at Brightfount's. Remember an objectionable little man called Seepage, who sometimes comes to see Mr B., saying to Gudgeon, 'This day-after-day business would never do for *me*. Can't think how you can stand it year after year.'

To which Gudgeon, whose general method of reply is to say nothing, remarked, 'You don't think of it year after year, you just take it day by day.'

Forget what Seepage said to that – something about never letting himself get caught in routine. When I get that feeling myself, always recall a French waiter mentioned somewhere in Arnold Bennett's Journals who had 'learned a whole philosophy in the practice of his vocation'. This is much better face to put on things than, for instance, Kafka's face. Did not get far with his Diaries: he groaned too much about going to the office every day.

MONDAY

I'll say this for Arch Rexine, he does encourage us to take an interest in things. Mr B. occasionally asks for suggestions, but nobody's ever known him act on them. Rexine will, though, in his own objection-able way. Some weeks ago, he asked us if we had any ideas for new selling lines. Dave, who is sold on that kind of thing, said, 'What about Space Travel and Flying Saucers?'

Rather to our amazement, Rexine agreed it was worth a try. Next thing we knew, great parcels arrived containing *Conquest of Space*, *Man on the Moon*, *Flying Saucers from Outer Space*, *Flying Saucers Are Real*, *Flying Saucers Have Landed*, *Flying Saucers on the Moon*, and so on. Dave was, to coin a phrase, shattered; but to-day – clearly having recovered – he virtually insisted on 'a Saucer window', as he calls it.

'It would be a waste of display space,' said Rexine grumpily.

Whereupon Dave showed us a letter in the *Journal and Advertiser* from someone claiming to have seen a saucer flying low over Bagger's Dune, a hill about four miles out of town. Dave said he thought it would be an incentive to sales.

So the saucers are in the window. Two sold during the day, so Dave may be right.

TUESDAY

Gudgeon is back from his summer holiday. He and a friend of his have been on the Broads – 'and in,' he said; 'we both fell in in turn.' We told him how brown he looked, but he said it was wind not sun. Wonder what he and his friend talked about, if they talked at all? We spend hours here in his company without ever feeling we really know him.

The great news to-day is another letter in the local paper about flying saucers from a man who writes, 'I was driving over the top of Bagger's Dune when the saucer came over, veered sharply south and looked as if it was going to land the other side of Dune Wood. Unfortunately I lost sight of it then.'

Dave elated. Sold more space books during day.

Did orders first thing, then spent rest of time clearing out Slaughterhouse. Mr B. is thinking of converting this shabby little den into what he ambitiously calls 'a print showroom'. First the outside wall will have to be rebuilt because the damp pours in. That will mean another invasion of workmen!

WEDNESDAY

Made fool of myself this morning. Customers don't always pronounce titles clearly and I suppose I had my mind on interplanetary visitors, etc. Anyhow, when I was asked for *Vivisection of the Universe*, I echoed the title in shocked amazement.

'I didn't say that at all,' the customer replied sharply. 'I asked for *Visual Perception of the Universe*.'

This slurring of words is misleading. Professor Carter asked Mrs Callow for a text of Beowulf once, and after a moment's thought she said, 'We've got *Br'er Rabbit*.'

Half-day. Went long cycle ride with Jack and Piggy Dexter. Kept one eye open for saucers. Had tea at charming place called 'The Red Jacket' (d/w to Stalin's works, perhaps?). Discovered terrific hornets' nest in rotten tree on way home.

Piggy said, 'Suppose the Martians or whoever they are landed just here. If they had never had to cope with insects before, the hornets would be quite invincible and the Martians would have to hop back to base and report that this planet was uninhabitable.' Hopeful thought.

THURSDAY

Thinking of changing digs; toast burnt again. Opened bed-room door to find landing thick with smoke. Tackled Mrs Yell about it and was told burning was due to poor quality of present-day bread: 'It don't stand up to flame like it used to.'

Arrived at shop feeling a little peevish.

Dull day. Gudgeon has got post-holidayitis and Dave pre-holiday-itis – he is off for a fortnight on Saturday. I had mine over Easter – too early. Continued in the Slaughterhouse, which is quite amusing, but after lunch had to sit and catalogue old Bohn editions of the classics; Mr B. wants to get out a special 'Cheap Only' stereotyped list by the end of next month. Shall these dry Bohns sell?

Heartily glad to slip out at five o'clock, pull off my tie and go round to meet Avril Dodd at the club. Played doubles with her against her brother Charles and old flame Helen. Good game. Went for a walk with her after; she's a bit solid but agreeable to talk to. Going to meet her again next Wednesday.

FRIDAY

Pay-day.

Forgot to say yesterday that space books are still selling. Dave and Rexine elated. To-day there was a third letter, anonymous, in the local paper at midday. The writer had actually seen 'two disc-shaped objects such as Adamski described in his book' floating over the Town Hall. They disappeared with an eerie whistling noise behind the Tastiped Shoe Factory.

'It's really getting quite alarming,' Peggy Ellis said nervously.

'I don't care if there's an entire Martian invasion,' Dave told her, 'provided we sell the books.'

'That's the spirit!' said Mr B., overhearing. He called down the cellar to Rexine, who was helping old Mr Parsons unpack parcels, 'You'd better order some more of those space books.'

Mrs Callow suggested – but *sotto voce* – that by the trend of things we might be wiser to stock up on the 'County Books' and guide books in case some Venusians materialize. Could not help visualizing what a revolution in the book trade, as in other spheres, a peaceful interplanetary invasion would cause. We should have a spate of *Venus in Pictures*, and there would be *Teach Yourself Venusian*, *Masterpieces of Venusian Art*, and as for travel books . . . The imagination – what's the exact word? – boggles.

Despite this excitement, I still sat in the back of the shop cataloguing Bohns. Emergency or not, what Mr B. says goes. Our dumb office wench, Edith, came downstairs about four to collect Rexine's post and said, 'Cheer up, things aren't as bad as you look.'

Several American tourists about; most of them are interested in buying prints – to compare with the photos they take, I suppose. Last year we had a Baltimore man in who told us what a lovely old town we had; Gudgeon, flattered beneath a stolid exterior, embarked on a description of the local antiquities.

'And one wall of St Mary's church dates back to about 1570,' he said proudly.

'Gosh, is that really so?' the visitor exclaimed. 'A.D. or B.C.?'

SATURDAY
Swim before breakfast. Very cold.

Always get odd people in shop on Saturday. Our 'thief' came in to-day – at least, we've suspected him for weeks but have never actually caught him. Everyone brightens up perceptibly when he comes in!

Dave very cheerful, last day at work and his saucer books going briskly. As we closed, Rexine said to him, 'You know I've ordered some more saucer books, don't you?'

'I know,' Dave said, 'but don't forget I shall be away next week. You'll have to carry on the job of writing fake letters to the Press or the sales may fall off.'

Takes his job seriously, does Dave – when it suits him.

SUNDAY

Found self quite looking forward to seeing Cousin Derek and wife. Odd of me really, because relations are never very exciting.

Got over to Graves St Giles earlier than usual. Derek and Myra were out in the car with Uncle Leo; apparently they are looking out for a house hereabouts, and Derek wants to motor to London every day.

Asked what Myra's sister was like.

'I thought you'd ask that!' says Aunt Anne coyly. 'Sheila is a very charming girl, and about your age. She left here on Friday to stay with some friends in Kent, but she may be back here next Sunday when you come.'

Inquired, not that I wanted to change the subject, after Uncle Leo.

'He seems to have been a little steadier since Derek arrived. But I fear he is undergoing a very odd phase just at present, very odd. You know my dear, I'm forced to say it, your uncle's not at all an easy person to live with.'

She looked rather tearful, so I hurriedly asked what effect Lawrence had had on him.

'Lawrence met your uncle when he was still at a very impression-able age. I'm sure he had a very profound effect on your uncle's ego. Now I am very far from being anything in the nature of a psycho-analyst, and heaven knows I could hardly be said to be even connected with the world of literature – not as much, even, as you are, Peter. The only thing I have ever had published – and this detail may amuse

31

you (even if you have heard it before) – was a knitting pattern. There used in my young days to be a monthly magazine called *Lady and Domicile*, defunct now, and they had this competition one Christmas . . . However, that was not what I was going to tell you.'

Aunt Anne has great strength of mind. She looks searchingly over the rose garden, as if to collect the lost thread of her narrative, and says, 'Lawrence had certain definite ideas about the human character, some of which were – and I say it without wishing to appear a prude – very unorthodox. He believed that every man should be an individual, and this deeply impressed your uncle. He is now trying to be an individual in the only way he knows: by being an eccentric.'

Had curious sensation of revelation listening to this. Aunt is quiet little woman, rather like one of Smollett's women, efficient, lively enough and without much depth. Now, sitting on the rustic seat listening to her, suddenly realized that all these years she had been watching Uncle Leo with acumen. Began, in fact, to feel nervous for Uncle, particularly if she had diagnosed wrongly.

At this point the car came up the drive. Uncle introduced me to Derek and Myra. Myra was very elegant and pleasant; Derek seemed a bit hearty. I can just remember him as very small boy running round pretending he had swallowed a balloon, to the consternation of Aunt Anne.

They drove me back here after tea.

MONDAY

Continued clearing out the Slaughterhouse. Miss Ellis and Gudgeon looked after the shop, but trade pretty slack; according to Gudgeon, only customer before eleven o'clock was a woman whose little girl required the nearest lavatory.

Main object of attack in the Slaughterh. to-day was Mr B.'s so-called 'reserve' desk – so-called because its drawers are so crammed with rubbish it is no longer usable; he abandoned it long ago for the one upstairs. He had to supervise the turning out; we filled a sack with waste. Every drawer bung-full with old correspondence and catalogues. No system, of course. One drawer contained nothing but

empty envelopes, addressed to 'Gaspin's' or 'Gaspin and Brightfount', which dates them a bit!

Other contents included loose chocolates, sealing-wax, a bottle of Vapex, early copies of *Criterion*, *Blast* and *London Opinion*, a mêlée of pencil stubs, two crushed cigars, an old pair of spectacles, some lino patterns, a photo of the shop, endless prospectusses and a box of pre-war cheese.

'We really ought to present this lot to the museum,' Mr B. said. 'Ah well, fling it out.'

The only things he did keep were some old rubber stamps and a faded photograph of Mrs Brightfount in a large, floppy hat.

Was laughing about the collection later to Mrs Callow. Gudgeon overheard and said, 'What's funny about it? A collection of miscellaneous articles is man's only defence against time.'

He makes some odd remarks occasionally.

TUESDAY

After last week's intensive campaign, interplanetary books are still selling well. *The Green and Red Planet* doing particularly nicely. Mrs Callow, leaning nonchalantly against the counter, informed me that she'd seen an announcement of the first book by a Martian pilot, entitled *One of Our Saucers is Missing*. Almost swallowed it.

Supposing these beings from another world arrived. Imagine them as dry, detached intellects in a sponge-like body; they casually present man with the secret of anti-gravity. In the succeeding outburst of space travel and planetary exploration, what an orgy of – not *adventure*, as the rocket-writers predict – but *learning* would follow! The barriers of every science would be broken down: geology, physiology, astronomy, chemistry, biochemistry, agriculture . . . What oddities of planetary architecture, to take geology, Mercury might yield, its airless plains eroded by lead streams and undermined by lava seas.

And biochemistry . . . in the great, gravity-less stations wheeling round the earth, white-coated men peer at their captive rats, rats conceived and born free of weight – rats the size of spaniels with brains accordingly enlarged.

There would be work for the publishers then, and of making many books less end than ever. *Some Unclassified Ganymedan Trypanosomes, Plutonian Oceanography, Alien Helminthology: with special reference to the parasites of Venusian Vertebrates*, would be unpacked at Brightfount's by some later-day Mr Parsons. A metal Mr Parsons perhaps.

A dream of learning – shattered maybe by the wail of sirens as telescreens announce, 'Attention earth, attention earth! Four space stations have been seized by the giant mutant rats, who even now prepare to drop H-bombs down on their creators!'

WEDNESDAY

Half-day. Spent the afternoon lazing in the sun, got cleaned up and met Avril at five. After (expensive) tea we watched dull cricket match on Poll's Meadow till stumps were drawn, when her brother Charles, who was playing, conscripted me for a match in a fortnight's time. Could not get out of it! Then Avril and I were making for a spot of peace and quiet when we ran into Piggy Dexter, who insisted on taking us into 'The Boar's Head' (dangerous pub name for Dr Spooner!).

Always expect to hear brilliant talk in pubs, perhaps with memories of Boswell at Child's. Generally disappointed – people have indisputably lost their fluency since Johnson's day, trained into passivity by radio and cinema. But one fragment charmed by its ambiguity: two men discussing a third as they left the bar, and one said, 'But the way he laughed! Do you think he was a bit high?'

'Oh no,' replied the other. 'I think he was genuinely amused.'

July nearly over! Ah me, in summer you forget it is not always summer and are consequently apt to forget to appreciate it to the full.

THURSDAY

Dave is having good weather for his holiday. Don't know where he is going – he didn't himself when he left on Sat. night. Said he was having a bookseller's holiday, i.e. could not afford to go away. Seems quiet in the shop without him; he's a bit rough, but good-hearted and good company. Think Peggy misses him. Mr B. is going to be away to-morrow, has to go into the country to look at a small library.

More remainders arrived to-day.

'Remainders are to the book trade what the Grand National is to bookies,' Mr Brightfount sometimes says; he loves a sweeping assertion as much as a gamble. His way of dealing with remainders is to 'spot a winner' and buy it all up, letting it sell slowly over the years.

Our cellar is encumbered with these lucky buys, so-called. There is *Ages at Bagger's Dune*, which being of local interests sells slowly: we are now down to the last two hundred copies. There is a study of Saxon cooking and table manners which seldom sells, called *Sir Gawaine at the Kitchen Door*. And there are stacks of copies of two memoirs by a doctor who worked for years in Poland which – most embitteringly when you think of the success of *Doctor in the House* and *Doctor at Sea* – never sell at all; these are *Fistulas on the Vistula* and its sequel, *Hand over Fistula*.

One of the most endearing features of book trade is its galaxy of titles, all gallimaufried together. Notice how many facets of human existence lie cheek by jowl in the booksellers' lists:

Carr, T. H., *Power Station Practice*
Carriage of Goods by Sea Act
Carroll, L., *Alice in Wonderland*
Cary, M., *A History of Rome*
Casanova, J., *Memoirs*

FRIDAY
Pay-day.

Likewise market-day. We were busy most of the morning with Dave and Mr B. away. Yesterday Arch Rexine put thirty duds from the Slaughterhouse on to our outside shelves; twelve of them sold before I went to lunch. A lot of Ruskins have gone. I've noticed before how old and rural-looking men buy Ruskin. These are folk unswayed by fashion. That's a thought which often worries me: aren't booksellers as much ruled by fashion as milliners? Inside or outside the head, the way of the world is the only way.

Queue of charabancs in Cross Street after lunch; trippers come specially to view the Castle. Mrs Callow said that once when she was on holiday at Eastbourne with her husband they went on a Mystery Tour and before they knew it were back here looking at the Castle!

'Hope you bought a guide?' Miss Ellis said.

'Not us. We slipped home to get a cup of tea and see if the cat was all right.'

SATURDAY

Dave is pretty illiterate, even for a bookseller's assistant. Had a card from him saying he was in London staying with a friend 'who is a bit of a rough daemon'. Conjures up an intriguing, mephistophelean figure. Surprisingly, Dave appeared while we were having tea break. He had had enough of London after looking round Foyle's and Charing X Road, and cycled home this morning. He cycles everywhere: next week he plans to do Reading, Oxford, Cheltenham, Birmingham. He visits all the bookshops. That's funny really, because you'd hardly call Dave a keen type.

Puzzle on the till roll this morning. I am a fool. During rush-hour yesterday I entered something that might be taken for either 'Agamemnon' or 'Afghanistan'; to-day I can neither decipher nor remember what it was. Rexine gave me level, evil stare, and said, 'I wonder if other bookshops have things like you?'

Had supper at Mrs Callow's; wish I had a landlady like her! Thought it friendly of Dave to come in and see us this morning, but there was an ulterior motive . . . on way back to digs met him in Park Road with Peggy Ellis, arm in arm. This is odd and no mistake! Wonder what Edith, our dumb office wench, would say? Always used to think she had a sort of rough affection for Dave.

August

SUNDAY

To-morrow is August Bank Holiday. Cannot afford to go home. Yet I do not mind the prospect of two days spent more or less on my own; solitude has pleasures no other state can bring. Generally something interesting arrives out of the blue to think about, or if it does not arrive, boredom which is unbearable in company is good for the soul alone.

Suddenly discover myself at such times, almost like a stranger – had been there all the time, but in the crowd had never noticed me.

Not spectacular day to begin August with, but about what might be expected: warm and cloudy, and the threat of rain. Cycled lazily out to Graves St Giles, taking the longer route through Upper Wickham. A few wild roses still in the tall hedges, but already the green blackberries show.

Ancient car passes me closely, hoots, brakes wildly. Out jumps Derek.

'Sling your bike in the back, old boy, and jump in. How do you like her, eh? Only bought her on Friday.'

Ask him what it is.

'A 1925 Cardiac. Sound as a bell. What do you think I gave for her?'

Say £20, which annoys him.

'Sixty – and that was devil's cheap. Move over, Myra, and let the blighter in!'

We cut through the village at a smart pace and slither up Uncle's drive in a cascade of gravel. Derek yells instructions to throw out the anchor, and we stop.

'How do you find Aunt and Uncle after all these years away from home?' I ask him as we go into the house.

'No different – a bit older, of course.' That is all he has to say; does he know nothing of the Lawrence legend, or is he merely insensitive? But at once Myra slips her arm through mine and says, 'And what a sweet, old-fashioned question it is for him to ask. And where has he been all his little life?'

Have no answer to this. Besides, she is very smart, has fringe and a pleasingly sharp look, and her arm (even offered in mockery) is not to be disdained. But Derek tells her angrily 'not to start that sort of stuff', and we go silently in to lunch. Myra winks at me once over the table.

Did not stay for tea.

Poured with rain before I got all the way back home. Soaked. Mrs Yell rather awkward about drying sports jacket.

AUGUST BANK HOLIDAY

Clouds cleared early. Should have liked day at the sea; the Callows were going to Bismouth on the nine o'clock coach.

Woke at 5.30 and could not get to sleep again. Had dreamed Brightfount's was forced to close because Mr B. could not induce us to be polite to customers. No matter how hard we tried, we broke into bitter outbursts of swearing when we began to serve anyone. Sounds funny now, but it was ghastly in the dream. Doubtless provoked by guilt complex; we are not always as absorbed in customers' inquiries as we should be.

Gudgeon's answer to anything is to 'look it up'. Often we see bored, fidgeting customers standing by while Gudgeon buries his nose in reference books. You can generally tell the sort that require only quick 'Yes' or 'No' reply. Poor old Gudgeon . . . he can be as portentous

40

over a fourpenny H.M.S.O. pamphlet as over a set of the Oxford Dictionary.

Dave's just the opposite; he'd rather make a good joke than a good sale.

These solemn thoughts provoked by reading *The Bankrupt Bookseller* in bed last night.

Went round to collect Avril Dodd after tea. Her parents have flat over their High Street shop – leather goods, handbags, trunks, etc. Very smart flat furnished in modern manner, uncomfortably low chairs, etc. Met Mr Dodd for first time: lean individual who looked rather a blighter, although he was affable enough. He was dressed ordinarily enough when I got there, but in a bit he disappeared and returned sporting a bright silk dressing-gown. He should meet Uncle.

Avril wanted to play tennis. I didn't, but gave in. Played with lanky female from Tastiped factory (think her name's Joy) against Avril and freckled chap from Midland Bank (forget his). Played best of three sets, Avril and bod winning. He bought us all ice-creams after.

Come to think of it, Avril looks rather like her Dad, although she is more solidly constructed: has sort of plump, sly look which is rather attractive. Kissed her for the first time.

'Bit public here, isn't it?' she said. 'Let's go home.'

Suitably squashed, took her home; but when we got there she produced latch-key and said, 'It's all right – they're out.' Blundered upstairs. It was getting dark. She gave me a warm hand and led me up to the sitting-room. At the door, she paused with her finger on the light switch, unconsciously silhouetting her bare arm against a fading square of window; kissed her again, now feeling considerably more sure of self.

When she flicked the light on, she allowed me another sidelong look and went to pour sherries for us. Took mine and sat politely on white chair; but she went over to a small sofa with sort of molecular pattern and thin legs and said, 'Come and sit by me.'

Muttered something foolish and went. A cold excitement made me almost slop the sherry. Sipped it and put it down, and then dared to look at her eyes. Burning bright. Took her into my arms.

In a little while – it might have been longer – we heard a key stab into the lock downstairs.

'Damn!' Avril said, and jumped up in a fluster. Her mother, father and another man came in, all looking rather grave, and apparently annoyed to find us. They attempted to be affable. Mr put the radiogram on, but I was fed up anyhow and left as soon as I could. Avril let me out into the street.

TUESDAY

Went back to work in a dream and served automatically most of day.

Could not sleep last night. After lying hopelessly in bed, I got up and crept downstairs, letting myself out of front door, terrified all the time that Gyp would bark. Even outside it felt stuffy. Hurried down the deserted streets; somewhere above me a television aerial clanked, although there was no wind. Passed into the High Street, empty, silent, and stood in front of Avril's shop.

Had expected nothing, yet was disappointed with nothing. Windows upstairs dark, window below reflecting the dress shop opposite, a pale mirage punctured by rows of handbags. No life anywhere.

Still feeling too exhilarated to go back, pushed on towards Cowpersgate and got free of the streets. A thin moon behind thin cloud was making a white night of it. Soon I stood by the court where she and I had played only a few hours ago: hooked my fingers into the guard netting for reality's sake and stared across the ground, trying to imagine her white figure.

All the excitement had left me now. Even Avril seemed to have faded, or I seemed to have her confused with 'Miranda', the sad-looking girl who bought a map two or three weeks ago. Why did she have to buy that, something to lead her away from Brightfount's?

Started back home. A badly tuned car snorted distantly towards the south; for all I knew it was Derek, belting for home in his bargain, caring for nobody but himself. Depressing thought. Slipped back into Mrs Yell's feeling really tired; as soon as I was in bed I was asleep.

WEDNESDAY

My first customer this morning: large, military lady with hearing aid who said, 'I'm looking for a suitable book to give as a present.' It seems to me there are many answers to that, but only asked her whom it had to suit.

'It's for a nephew of mine. He's a Communist architect interested in the theatre.'

Marx? Bannister Fletcher? Allardyce Nicoll? No . . . She left with a P. G. Wodehouse.

Half-day. No sign of Avril in any of her usual haunts. Hung about till 3.30 before realizing how I was wasting time. Went long walk by self via canal and right through Stagford woods. Wet but marvellous. Two years since I last went that way; can't think why. Should be good year for conkers!

THURSDAY

Letter from Mother. 'We missed you a great deal over the Bank Holiday. Enclosed is your railway fare to come home with on Saturday.' Don't at present particularly want to go home.

Grand old chuck out from Topog. section upstairs. We were all on it except Mrs C., who was busy typing lists, and Peggy Ellis, who was set to mind the shop – oh, and Gudgeon who dislikes exertion. Glorious job, coats off, dust so thick you could hardly see across room! Enter Peggy in flap, says, 'There's a whole crowd of foreigners just come in,' obviously expecting us to hurry down and cope.

Mr Brightfount straightened up, polished the dust off his specs and remarked calmly, 'Well, you don't have to be frightened of them. They'd be English, you know, if they hadn't been born on the other side of the Channel.'

Shrewd point there. I was sent to help, but they only wanted postcards.

Poured with rain and thundered in afternoon. Visit from one sad, soaked traveller, 'just passing through'. Rexine saw him, ordered one copy of one title. Remarked that I should not mind working in London. He said, 'Don't you. It's full of blackguards and placards.'

Personally I always love the hoardings and adverts. Remember last time I was up there (Festival of Britain?), saw the sign of Universal Aunts Ltd. Intriguing name! The man from the public library had an odd circular the other day – from some people calling themselves Nomenclature Ltd. He brought it round to show Mr B. Part of it read: 'Eighty-five thousand unused classified titles available. Authors! Journalists! Publishers! A good title *sells* your work.' And right across the sheet their slogan, 'We name Anything'.

This seems to me the very latest and best of literary rackets. Wonder what they would have suggested if Shakespeare had written in and said he wanted a title for Hamlet? Maybe *Tonight, Sweet Prince*. And how many of our modern masterpieces might not be known under different names if this firm had been operating thirty years ago! Think of *The Specialist* as *Sitting Room Only* and *Ulysses* as *The Bloomsday Book* . . .

If they undertake the naming of abstract art they must have plenty of scope!

FRIDAY
Pay-day.

Pretty busy, it being market-day. Mrs Callow was up in attic most of time, turning off Cheaps List on the Gestetner.

Mentioned Nomenclature Ltd. to her. She said they could not improve on her favourite title in the Rolls series. Thought of those formidable dull brown tomes and asked in bewilderment: Which? She said, 'Thomas Saga Erkibyskups'. A name indeed not to conjure with. Erkibyskups – pure Lear!

It was pouring with rain as we closed, but having seen nothing of Avril all week I went round to hers. Mrs Dodd answered door and said with blank face that Avril could not come out. My face must have gone equally blank, because her manner softened and she said, 'You may as well know, because you're bound to hear about it later, but we have hit a patch of trouble. That's why Avril can't come.'

Cannot understand this. Perhaps it's just an excuse. Wrote Avril unsatisfactory sort of note to drop in to-morrow morning.

SATURDAY
Dreary day again to-day. Hope for a blazing to-morrow.

Jocelyn Birdwine appeared and paid his account. Rexine was getting worried about it. Am always delighted to see Birdwine – he is most eccentric of all our regular customers. Appeared to-day in shorts and sandals, had just arrived back by banana boat from south of France. He said he wanted recent book on sex whose title he had forgotten, but the blurb said 'Will appeal alike to the specialist and general reader'.

In the end he paid four pounds for Howard's *Early English Drug Jars*. Such a romantic title! There's no one I would prefer to have it.

SUNDAY
Spent – no, too tired to bother to write this evening.

MONDAY
Spent quite a good day yesterday, but somehow returned to work this morning feeling rather depressed; parents had felt obliged to hold inquiry on what Father calls 'my future prospects'. It began soon after breakfast with Mother asking me how much I got paid each week. Told her. Mother: 'It doesn't sound enough for a bright boy like you. You always did so well at school – have you told Mr Brightfount how well you did?' Father: 'Dash it, Monica, you talk to the boy as if he were still a – well, boy. He's twenty-five now, don't forget.' But as if there might nevertheless be *something* in what she said, he turns on me and says, 'Do *you* think you're getting enough?'

Only one answer to that question.

So they both begin talking . . . Getting on in Life . . . Need for Initiative . . . Thought to the Future . . . Sacrifice of Career on Altar of Books . . . The vision of this unstable edifice makes me laugh. 'I'm dead serious,' says F. angrily, asks about forthcoming prospects.

Tell him: 'Almost every week the leading booksellers and publishers have meetings and discuss ways of making more money, not only for themselves but for their assistants. V. kind, noble bunch of men. These discussions have continued for *years*.'

Reported conv. later to Mrs Callow, who remarked ambiguously, 'All parents hate to see that their swan has turned into a goose.' Which reminds me of the time we bought a large bird book off a customer who said to Mrs Callow, 'I'm glad to get rid of it – it's very dull.'

'Ah,' exclaimed Mrs Callow. 'Yawnithology!'

TUESDAY

Dave back from his holiday to-day – had an extra day to make up for the Bank Holiday. Just completed cycle tour of Cheltenham and Oxford district, sleeping at the home of an old army friend. He called in on several bookshops whose names we know well either from *Clique* or from invoice tops. He said in most places the assistants brightened up considerably when they found he was not a customer, just a mut like themselves. Verdict on Oxford: traffic ghastly, cafés worse, bookshops 'marvellous' – 'but rum lot of nuts serving in them who probably didn't know how lucky they were.' Thought of such big shops suddenly seemed to raise Dave's ire. 'They ought to jolly well come and work here!' he said.

'That's advice you might take yourself,' interrupted Arch Rexine unkindly, appearing briskly out of his office. We duly 'got on with it'.

Workmen in shop again. Always seem to be workmen here – this time they are decorating Slaughterhouse. Looks like being long job, judging at least by the lack of enthusiasm with which they began work.

Also road up just outside – slow queues of buses and cars up and down Cross Street.

More I see of our senior assistant Gudgeon, less I understand him. With air of proud modesty he has just produced complicated analysis of one of yesterday's till rolls. We have two tills, one for new books (including remainders) only, the other for everything else – second-hand, prints, stationery, etc.; these tills are known respectively as News and Stews. Gudgeon 'analysed' Stews. Total takings were £13 19s. 6d., earned over 34 transactions; of these, 15, or nearly half, the customers gave correct change, but these 15 transactions only represented £3 19s. 3d. or about 28 per cent of total takings. Of the 15 customers giving correct change, 10 were women.

'Just exactly what does all that prove?' asked Dave.

Gudgeon shrugged. I sometimes wonder if he likes Dave very much. 'Quite a lot,' he said; 'shows the time we waste. Even after the books which that £3 19s. 3d. represents were virtually sold, we spent over half an hour standing watching hands fiddling about in handbags and fingers pingling about in purses. Say there's the same wastage on the other till, that's *fifteen days* lost on such helpfulness every year. Staggering, eh?'

'How long do we take to give change?' I asked.

'And what's the remedy?' Miss Ellis asked.

Surprisingly, Gudgeon had an answer for her. He said that publishers were partly to blame: they priced books at 9s. 6d. or 10s. 6d., why was the fashion against the round ten bob? He said it made his blood boil to think of all those dainty, gloved fingers niggling hopelessly about for odd sixpences at the publishers' dictates.

Wonder how he'd like to deal in fabric lengths at 16s. 11¾d. per yard? Of course he has always had morbid preoccupation with time, poor old boy.

Always have high tea with the Yells now, instead of upstairs alone – pleasant arrangement, especially for Gyp, who is partial to snacks. Got back to-day to find letter with local postmark awaiting me; it could only be from Avril. Wished then could have been by myself in my room to read it, as Mrs Yell was obviously bursting for me to open it.

'It's not from your mother,' she said.

'No.'

'Nor your Aunt Doris at Colchester.'

'No.'

'Looks like a lady's handwriting though.'

'Them kippers'll be burnt,' warns Mr Yell, and reluctantly she retreats to the kitchen.

It *was* from Avril, one of those horrible ambiguous notes women will send. It said, 'I am sure you cannot think much of me. I do not think much of myself, I can tell you that, dear. So perhaps what has happened is just as well. Please do not try and make a fuss, because I would not want that.

'The cricket match is still on to-morrow and Charles will be playing. I will see you then to say good-bye.

Yours,
Avril.'

Could not make it out. We had not quarrelled. What did she think had happened? Or if she knew, why did she not tell me straight out?

Got that wretched kipper down somehow and then went out; was determined to see what exactly it was all about. Hurried down High Street and drew up in front of their shop. For the once, the blinds were down: across each pane of glass was plastered a red notice which bore the words, 'These Premises Have Been Sold'.

Went slowly back the way I had come.

WEDNESDAY
Half-day.

Notice appeared beside tills first thing: Please Give Incorrect Change. Gudgeon removed same without comment, but not without a forbidding glance at Dave. All very till-conscious; even Peggy Ellis entered everything on right tills.

Odd customer in; came to collect copy of *Grinding of Steel* which we had ordered for him. Stared at it in horror and said he must have made a mistake, thought it was a thriller, did not know it was a technical book. Title misled him. No sale.

Also having trouble with customer called Hasluck, only in his case we are on to the right book but just can't get hold of it for him. He came in again to-day and it was not here – but even that did not cheer me up!

Were just closing when Mr B. appeared from upstairs and called me. I did not seem to be my normal cheerful self just lately; even Mr Rexine had noticed it. Was there anything wrong? Could he give any assistance or advice?

Could only say no, but left feeling pretty staggered that old Rexine should have noticed anything like that.

Cricket match was due to start at 2.45. We went out to field at about half-past three; rain delayed play. There were several showers throughout game, and wicket was beastly.

Bishops Linctus XI made 82 all out and we won by two wickets. I got five runs – and missed a *sitter* at mid on. Was glad when it was all over, really, Avril having appeared during last few minutes.

Charles was still getting his pads off, so we dodged him. Poor Avril! Her father has gone bust, not over the shop but through some reckless work on the Stock Exchange. The shop has to be sold up to meet creditors' demands.

Apparently this has happened twice before, once when Avril was a babe, once just after World War II. Directly he gets in funds again he cannot resist dabbling. All this I heard at great length interspersed with a few tears. It began to rain steadily and we had to shelter under canal bridge.

Remember that evening at Dodd's, Mr came in with a man who was saying something about disposal of stock. Now Mrs Dodd refuses to leave the house, says she is too ashamed to be seen, and they all go to some relatives of hers up in Huddersfield *next Saturday*!

Much shivering and sniffing from Avril, but soon managed to comfort her. It gets dark quite early these evenings.

THURSDAY

Rooting round our Lit. shelves, grunting and mumbling to himself as usual, was Boris Maclaren. We keep away as much as possible, terrified of him. He is much worse since *Picture Post* did a feature on him two years ago ('Scholar-author on Century-old Houseboat Home'), calling him 'The Man Who Makes History Exciting'. That was just after he'd been here making our life partic. exciting and nearly got Dave the sack. ('If I ever come across that houseboat, I hope I've got a brace-and-bit with me,' said Dave darkly, when we saw the article.)

Now Maclaren looks as if he wants also to be The Man Who Makes Literature Readable. From our various points of concealment we heard him tell Rexine he was going to prune Proust – cut it by two-thirds – knock it into proper chronological order, etc., etc.

'Prune Proust indeed,' snapped Mrs Callow when he had gone. 'He doesn't want a bookshop, he wants an ironmonger's – they'd sell him a pair of secateurs.'

FRIDAY
Pay-day.

SATURDAY
Ghastly noise every day now from road-menders outside. Pneumatic drill going intermittently, concrete mixer all the while. Makes those indistinctly murmured titles even harder to hear.

Usual Sat. afternoon crowd hanging about, not buying as much as you'd expect. Also the plump man we call our thief, comes in every week, highly suspish. Suppose such people must be permanent and traditional feature of book trade, just as Maclaren is. Ah well, no trade is perfect.

Nipped round in lunch-hour to say farewell to Avril. Quite an anti-climax in its way, because was half-prepared to find her weepy and dramatic. Instead she was horribly cheerful: her parting words, in fact, were, 'I've got some handsome male cousins in Huddersfield.'

Good luck to 'em, by gum!

SUNDAY
Pouring with rain all morning, so decided not to go out. The Yells were not in, so had nothing for lunch but three bits of Ryvita with crab paste on. Reading Jacquetta Hawkes' *A Land* – really absorbing – so quite happy.

But it cleared up about two, so got my bike out and rode over to 'Hatchways' to make sure of a decent tea. Arrived to find Uncle and Aunt having desultory sort of argument with Derek and Myra. Uncle has always been afraid of the house being burgled if left empty, consequently he and Aunt Anne have not had a holiday since before the 1939-45(6?) war. Now Derek is here to occupy it, he is trying to make Uncle go away, although in unpleasant fashion.

'Well, we're offering you the chance!' he exclaims. 'Offer'll be withdrawn once we get a place of our own.'

'I don't want to go,' says Uncle, rather miserably.

'What are you afraid we'd do? Throw wild parties here?'

'No, of course not. I just don't want to go.'

Can tell by Aunt's face that although she dislikes Derek's methods of persuasion she hopes they'll succeed.

Derek goes over to the phone, picks up the receiver, dials 'O' and says over his shoulder, 'I'm going to get on to the Grand at Folkestone and fix up a double room for you straight away.'

Myra says to him, lightly and pleasantly, 'You realize, of course, that you are behaving like a pig?'

He drops the phone and says, 'Oh, hell, they must please themselves then – I was only doing it for their sakes.' And there the matter was left.

MONDAY

Oh, how some queries hang on and hang on! Was sickened to find that our first customer of the week was the little bald man called Hasluck. Personally, he is very pleasant, accepts our apologies with a cheerful, 'Please don't mention it at all!' – but he has been the object of a Query for the past month, and as such we begin to hold even his affability against him. You only have to say 'Hasluck' now and the whole staff trembles.

'Good morning! Has it come in this morning?' he asks lightly (but I catch a certain dogged determination in his voice).

'I'll see,' I say, retreating to Order Shelves in Rexine's office. Hasluck no longer has to name his book, we all know it so well, and him so well. Soothing to think he also knows us well and must be sick of us and our bright promises.

'So sorry, it's not in yet, Mr Hasluck,' I say. I knew without looking, but he has to be humoured.

'Oh that's all right – I just happened to be passing . . . I'll come in again to-morrow, shall I?'

Exit Hasluck. 'If only he'd be *rude* about it,' sighs Dave, who has watched from shelter of World Classic display.

The book in question is *Glimmering Landscapes*. Alas for us, Hasluck – not a booky type – met the author; it was his first author; he decided he'd like a copy of the book. He came into Brightfount's and ordered it. *Glimmering Landscapes*: poetical autobiographical travel, the sort of book that comes two a penny on any publisher's list. Report came back – Out of Print.

Peggy Ellis had taken the order, but when Edith, our dumb office wench, went to type the report, she misread Hasluck for Auslich, an American customer of ours, and he was duly informed 'Regret *Glimmering Landscapes* no longer obtainable: out of print.'

When Hasluck called, his card was found – but without the report. Nobody thought to ask Edith, so we had to start again. Again, O/P, reported after ten days.

This Hasluck gently denied, said 'author told him lots of copies on sale in Bristol', etc. We wrote in desperation to the obvious shop in Bristol, who reported their stock came from an obscure remainder dealer up North. We wrote there. No answer.

Arch Rexine, cornered by Hasluck in the shop, actually telephoned and was told 'Sorry, binding. Should be ready in a week.' That was a fortnight ago.

TUESDAY
Spent nearly all day precariously balanced on ladder on stairs, dictating details of books on Ancient History (incl. Classical) to Mrs Callow for our next catalogue.

WEDNESDAY
Thumping a patent breakfast cereal which looked like a battered flock mattress in front of me, Mrs Yell said, 'I can't manage no porridge this morning, ducks. Mr Yell ain't well, and when he ain't well he's a proper handful.'

She had the air of one who has suffered the Final Blow. As it was half-day, I went to see her husband after lunch. He was in bed, but propped up and cheerfully smoking his pipe. 'Only a touch of malaria,' he said, 'Picked it up in the Dardanelles in the first war, you know. Does me a world of good to have it – creates a bit of sympathy, like, in the proper quarters.'

The Proper Quarters appeared in a minute and chased Gyp off the foot of the bed. 'Just imagine – dogs in a sick room!' she exclaimed in disgust.

'Do you want me to leave?' I asked, thinking she was going to make his bed.

'Oh I didn't mean you!' she said. 'You aren't doing no harm.'

When she had gone, Mr Yell started telling me about the first World War; after a bit, I read to him for a couple of hours a saga of the second war: *The Cruel Sea*. This was a copy he said someone had given him last Christmas, but he does not read v. fast.

Took his old dog out for a walk afterwards. Gyp is real out-and-out mongrel: or would it be kinder to call him a canine anthology? Went just up Bishop's Hill and along High Street. Could not resist having a look at that empty shop, blinds drawn, upper windows blank. And on the door and windows those curt, red notices still.

THURSDAY

Man from the paper mill in this morning, down in the cellar consulting with Mr B. and old Mr Parsons over corrugated cardboard, etc. Likeable chap, but with what I call 'the Army manner' – can never forget he was in the Services. Still makes barrack-room jokes he must have been making for years, but told quite amusingly all the same. Had one about a sergeant-major announcing on morning parade, 'Lecture in the Drill' All at 18.30 hours on Keats. I daresay as some of you ignorant devils don't know what a Keat is, but you'll find out to-night.' Quite a good variation on an old theme.

Mr Parsons rather grumpy just lately. For one thing, we are a little slack at pres., few parcels going out, and Mr P. is good packer and enjoys doing it. For another, the cross-eyed carpenter Vaws and his mate are engaged in shelving Slaughterhouse. This causes more dirt in shop for Mr P. to clean up ('That bloke Vaws spreads more muck than a chimney-sweep,' he told Rexine). The carpenter's wood is stored in the cellar – in Mr P.'s way – and there, too, frequent brew-ups of tea take place – to Mr P.'s disgust.

He should feel better next week. Our Cheaps List was sent out to-day: we ought to get a few orders by next Tuesday.

FRIDAY
Pay-day.

Got quite a bit more work done on Ancient Hist. catalogue.

Poor old Hasluck in first thing. Gudgeon got him. Hasluck affable, half-apologetic as usual. Still no book.

'We'll send you a card when it comes,' Gudgeon told him. 'That'll save you keeping coming in. You'll get the thing no quicker by calling on us every day.'

'I don't know how you could be so unkind to the poor little fellow,' Dave said when Hasluck had gone.

'Nonsense,' our senior assistant replied grumpily. 'Can't have customers getting out of hand. Besides, if he suffers a bit for this book he'll appreciate it all the more.' There may be something in this idea. Supposing we made book-buying harder instead of easier? Would not this create a demand, human nature being what it is?

Visions attended me in afternoon of a book rationing system that would make the yearly 13,000 new books or whatever it is a scarcity instead of, honestly, a glut. ('I'm afraid this coupon doesn't entitle you to a whole Mee's *Children's Encyclopaedia*, madam; but we can do you a volume of the *Oxford Junior*'. Or, 'No sir, these white ones are only valid for paper-backs. You have to forfeit two of the mauve coupons for a cloth-bound edition.' Or, 'Sorry, we cannot accept Book Tokens until you produce a certificate from your oculist.' Or even, 'The queue on the far side of the shop is for art books, madam; at present you're in the queue for Black Market Bibles.')

British Road Services arrived late, just as I was going off for lunch. They brought one book, *Glimmering Landscapes* – the book Mrs Callow now refers to as 'Hasluck's Folly'. Gudgeon duly sent a card.

Was just about to pop into Fletcher's café when I realized that Uncle Leo was walking along ahead of me. Never noticed before how small he is. He held a brief case and was walking briskly with thin shoulders squared in quite a military manner; but he looked terribly alone, and far too fragile and aged to be alone. Caught up with him and spoke to him.

'Very nice to see you, Peter,' he said. 'I am so excited. Do you know I've decided to take Anne down to the seaside?'

'Not – Folkestone?'

'Folkestone and none other!'

'But I thought you were against the idea?'

'Oh I was, but there were some business matters needing clearing up then; now everything's settled and I can go away with a free heart. You may as well be the first to know – I've changed my name!'

'Whatever for?'

'You mean "whatever to?" I've changed it to Aldys, A-L-D-Y-S. Don't you think it's a great improvement on "Aldiss"? Why it's now quite noble enough to stand by Pepys or Knollys. Do spread the news round, won't you?'

Heard more about the change of name to-day.

Uncle has been doing research and has found that a man called John Aldyn subscribed £25 towards the defence of his country against the Spanish Armada in 1588. He presumes this was an ancestor; hence the change – but to Aldys rather than Aldyn just because he thinks the one sounds better than the other.

Aunt merely says it's a bit late in life for her to be changing her name again, but is quite cheerful because they are off to Folkestone next Saturday.

'You can come back here while we're away,' she offers.

'Oh, do!' says Myra. 'That would be fun!'

Manage to find excuses.

Heard Dave greeted brightly by Edith, our dumb office wench. 'Saw you and your girl friend yesterday,' she said. 'You were just off for a preamble in the woods.' Mrs Callow also overheard this malapropism, confessed it made her grin all over her preface.

Wonder if the girl friend was Peggy? Somehow don't think so – or else they disguise it pretty well in shop hours.

Strenuous day putting books away. Need a shoe-horn to get another book into Biography now. Five sets of Morley's *Gladstone*! Our case looks hopeless with them wedged in the middle of it.

Some days the sense of the past trapped in our old volumes gives me a sensation like choking; feel I must liberate those spirits by reading their works, or at least flick over the stiff pages in an effort to assuage the print's need for eyes. That unopened set of Landor over the Topog. Room door! The seventeen vols. of Lord Byron gathering dust outside Mr B.'s office! But humanity is so busy . . . even in Brightfount's we do a fair amount of work. Some days, I wish Brightfount's would up and fly away with us in it to remote and distant places where no customers could disturb: then we could just lie back and read and read.

Other days – and so to-day – I just feel sick of the sight of books. Brightfount's could up and fly away on its own and I should not worry. All these outpourings of dead minds seem merely abhorrent.

Yet how delightful to be becalmed in a schooner on the South Seas and notice, floating on the blue water, waves lapping gently at its steps, Brightfount's! A staid old English ark upon a sea of sunshine! To set forth in a dinghy for the Local History . . . O rest ye, brother mariners, we will not labour more.

We look prosaic enough in Cross Street: moored off Papeete or the Santa Cruz Islands we should stand out for the exciting place we really are. But there – I expect there's a clause against it in the Net Book Agreement.

Return to reality and sell a lady picture postcard of west front of Cathedral.

Back to digs to find Mr Yell up and about again and pleased with himself.

TUESDAY

Subdued groans from staff as Ralph Mortlake entered. Mr Brightfount managed to slip upstairs in time. Mortlake, besides being reviewer, has recently been appointed drama critic on local paper; his manner is suitably theatrical. This morning he wanted a second-hand copy of MacQueen-Pope's *Ghosts and Greasepaint* we had in the window.

'Sold it on Saturday,' Dave said contentedly.

Melodramatically, Mortlake clutches his heart. 'Foiled,' he groans.

('A very famous bookshop,' whispers Mrs Callow.)

He hangs about shop until Mr B. incautiously descends, then says he will bring in some more review copies for us to buy. Mr B. hedges, finally says O.K. So in the afternoon we get another trunk full of tripe and a long haggle over its value, as if there could be any real doubt about that.

If you are second-hand bookseller, the great task is not to *get* books but to keep them away. Every week we get all sorts of rubbish thrust at us; if we took it all our roof would sink below foundations.

It is really staggering what junk people harbour – even more staggering the way they bring it in and expect it to be worth something. Odd volumes, incomplete sets, coverless books, books with pages missing, nineteenth-century Bibles, twentieth century Dickenses . . . all assuredly worth a fortune! And some people get quite annoyed when told they could do nothing better than throw it out.

Mortlake's articles have titles like 'What Interests Me About Brighton', 'Why I Made an Unhappy Marriage', 'How I Cured My Athlete's Foot', 'Where I Put My Cacti'. His review books are of the same kind, more calculated to please for a moment than last for a week.

Forward, not permanent, sweet, not lasting,
The perfume and suppliance of a minute.

Mr B. prods them over rather disapprovingly. He is marvellous at buying books second-hand, with just the right mixture of tolerance and sternness to persuade customers that, however little he gives them, he will make small profit himself. Mortlake of course is used to the gambit and says hopefully at intervals, as a particularly gaudy jacket is passed, '*That* was a good one. *That* was a good one.'

Towards the end of the pile, Mortlake grows more voluble, Mr B. more taciturn. Finally the latter names his price.

'Only three ten? Is that an offer or an aspersion?' gasps M. 'Can I believe my unhappy ears? Only three ten?'

Magnificently, Mr B. unbuttons his jacket, looks squintwise down at a row of pens clinging like barnacles to his inner pocket, selects a bright green one, and commences to write a cheque. 'Only three ten,' he says.

WEDNESDAY

More work on Ancient History – managed to finish it!

Had charming American visitor in, who asked if we had any books on coffin-making, cemetery-planning, body-snatching, Resurrection Day, 'or kindred material'. All I could find was *Monumental Brasses of North Devon*, which would not do. The customer chatted genially for a while. Before leaving he showed me his card: he was a Los Angeles funeral director. On the other side of card was a repro. of an ancient cartoon from *Punch*, showing seedy undertaker bearing a placard with the words: 'Starved out Undertakers. People won't die and we can't live.'

Went slow walk with Mr Yell before tea. He much preoccupied with scarcity of groundsel and price of canary seed.

THURSDAY

More Americans in to-day. Charming people; terribly solemn, though! At least, the married ones seem most solemn. Had in a gay bachelor from Washington, D.C. Sold him splendid facsimile of John Kip's

View of London and Westminster in twelve sheets, and signed copy of *Your Poodle Right or Wrong*.

Arch Rexine told him story about an American customer who came in and asked us for signed first edition of Sophocles, which amused good-natured visitor very much. Odd thing about this is that I told Rexine that story long time ago, only he has it slightly wrong: it was an early American bookseller selling the Sophocles to ignorant millionaires, and the whole thing was an incident in a novel I read called *Tobias Brandywine*.

But Rexine really believes what he says. Have often heard him tell the story his way.

FRIDAY

Pay-day, on strength of which had haircut in lunch-hour. Long wait there; only just had time for snack before getting back to shop. Chap cutting my hair was Jugoslav, seemed content with amount of freedom in England. Talk somehow got round to books. He said, 'When I come here, for learn English I buy three books, but is very hard to learn. Best way for learn foreign language is not by books, is by girls. Then you have the interest.'

Amusing and true, although bad for the poor old book trade. 'French without a Master' impossible without a mistress.

Mr B. out most of afternoon buying small local library of books. Meanwhile Dave and I, with some dignified assistance from Gudgeon, struggled to put last buy away.

Rexine sold old, pre-war edition of *Encyclop. Brit.* just before closing. He's generally pretty laconic salesman until he feels sure of a customer, then he is full of zest. He pulled the heavy red vols. off the shelf, scattering dust liberally and talking all time: 'Much better than latest edition . . . No good nowadays – all science . . . They knocked two pages off Beethoven when jets were invented. Greek Art had to go to make room for Geiger counters,' etc., etc. All highly inaccurate, but the spirit's there, and we carted the set triumphantly out to a car.

Rexine v. affable after, said 'Good night' to everyone.

SATURDAY

Lot of customers in, not much selling. Row of last-century Baedekers put on outside shilling shelf have all gone – in one week!

Rexine even more affable to-day. Mr B. packed up at noon, cheerfully said good-bye to us all and is off for week's holiday. Rained most of afternoon, but hoped this only wetted his appetite.

August–September

Am writing this outdoors for a change. Wonderful afternoon, the sun at its sweetest. Lucky old Mr B.! I lie in field by the river, propped dozily against an old willow tree, Gyp beside me, snoring slightly in the short grass.

Not everything ages as beautifully as willows. After a prim youth, they break into a gnarled fantasy of shape. This one has split, hinged and curved; its pruned topknot has sprouted canes in all directions, some pointed high, some within inches of Gyp's nose. It has twisted away from an imaginary centre like a banana unpeeling itself and looks as little like a normal tree as possible.

If I turn my head back slightly, my eye travels up the grey bark and I become a minute being walking up a rutted road. Alarming precipices fall away on either side, the surface sprouts huge poles with green flags on them, while further on it becomes a hill whose slope I climb until the part I trod before hangs far below me. Then there is a road block; great mesas of bark pile up; out of them grows a vibrating green bridge that stretches over the water.

It would be terrifying to be as small as that – so small that to tread in one drop of dew might mean having one's leg caught in a globe of great elasticity and suction. Or to be even smaller, a gnat, when a dewdrop on a leaf would look like one of the glassite domes moon explorers erect in Dave's space stories, a glassite dome on a trembling green plain!

Quite arbitrary, when you think of it, this business of being on an average about six feet tall. Some races of pygmies only stand about four feet high. What accident prevents us being two feet high? The world would seem a vastly different place – impossible to visualize just how different, except in obvious ways. Possibly, despite such puny stature, we might still have managed to capture wild horses, but our steeds would be Great Danes and Alsatians. Had we once managed to survive the magnified dangers of a primeval environment, our smallness might prove a positive advantage. Less material would have to be grown and quarried to provide clothes and housing, less food would be needed for smaller stomachs. Should we have crossed the Atlantic yet? – and if so, how high is a skyscraper?

On the whole, providing there weren't too many of us, it would be much more interesting to be vastly bigger rather than vastly smaller. Being as tall as a coconut palm has certain obvious advantages, especially in a land of coconut palms. If we had a poorer view of the daisies of the field, we should have a better view of the horizon. And I could use my willow then as a buttonhole.

MONDAY
Mysterious beckonings from behind Art case by Peggy Ellis. Glancing at one or two customers loitering about shop, I joined her and asked if anyone was pinching anything.

'No, it isn't that,' she said. 'You see the lady up there with the white gloves on? . . . Bet you a man with dark wavy hair joins her in a minute.'

Was serving someone else when he appeared, a harassed, pleasant-looking chap who at first took no notice of the lady in white gloves. Gradually he worked his way past the cheap editions, running a finger along a shelf, until he was close to her. They spoke quietly together for ten minutes, walking unostentatiously about the shop and then leaving separately without a touch of the hand – only a lightening of the eyes.

We were better able to discuss this matter thoroughly as not only was Mr Brightfount away on holiday, but Arch Rexine was busy arguing about new shelves with the carpenter in the Slaughterhouse. Dave thought the pair were crooks operating on a grand scale and secretly observing our movts. before pinching every book in the shop. Scorn from Mrs Callow, who said obviously they were lovers. I agreed: they had met by the poetry section.

'They came in just like that on Saturday,' Peggy said. 'Gazed all round the shelves in an odd sort of way and then went out without saying anything.'

The episode quite brightened our day; after all, we lead very secluded lives.

TUESDAY

Orders beginning to roll in from our recent Cheaps List. Kept me fairly busy all morning.

Definite holiday feeling creeping in with Mr B. away, despite Rexine's attempts to lash us to greater efforts. Dave spent half an hour down cellar chatting to Mr Parsons. Mr Parsons' nephew bought an old Steam Traction engine for £50 recently and news of this machine thrills Dave more than anything.

Sold quaint little old ed. of La Rochefoucauld's Maxims today. Text printed in red, but all punctuation including apostrophes in green. There have been some odd books printed in odd ways!

WEDNESDAY

More orders. Quite a pile of mail to-day from all over world. Romantic really how it converges from the four corners onto Brightfount's. Actually very little business seems to amount from it all, most correspondents wanting cheap copies of unheard of or scarce books. Remember Mr B. once referred to the mail as 'the impecunious in search of the unprocurable'.

Always loathe publishers at this time of year. While ordinary people are trying to prolong summer, they eagerly proclaim autumn. Autumn! – I ask you!

Back to digs to find postcard with view of Folkestone resting against my plate. It said: 'Greatly enjoying ourselves, nice comfy hotel. May stay on for three weeks depending on weather. Your Uncle behaving almost normally. Love, Aunt A.'

Read it and stuffed it uncomfortably in pocket, sure I was not the only one in the house who had read it.

'Have a good day at the business?' Mr Yell asks.

'Yes. Pretty busy.'

'Um – nice looking view on your postcard,' says Mrs Yell. 'Couldn't help just glancing at it as I brought it in off the mat.'

'Of course.'

'Seaside, wasn't it?'

'Folkestone.'

'Ah. Very nice spot, I believe.'

'Knew a bloke came from there once,' says Mr Yell, doing his best to divert her. 'He was with me in the Mules in the Dardanelles.'

'Let's see,' says Mrs Y. 'Didn't you say your Uncle and Auntie out at Graves had gone there to stay?'

'To the Dardanelles?'

'No, no, to Folkestone.'

'Oh . . . yes, actually the card was from my Aunt.'

'I *see*. Is she having a good time?'

'She seems to be.'

'And your *Uncle*?'

'She says they're both enjoying themselves very much.'

'There's another sausage in the frying pan,' suggests Mr Yell. 'It shouldn't be too cold, if you want it.'

'You never say much about your Uncle,' Mrs Yell persists. 'Did he have to go there for health reasons, dear?'

'Yes,' I tell her. 'He was nearly going off his nut.'

THURSDAY

Lo and behold, lovers in shop first thing. She passed him envelope, he wrote something on the back of it and stuck it in his pocket, so now Dave suggests he may be blackmailer. We may never see them again and never learn the truth, which is horribly tantalizing. Feel there is a short story behind this episode.

Poor old Gaspin came in during the afternoon. He must be about ninety-five, owned Brightfount's long before the war. Still likes to keep an eye on the old place. Not more than five years ago he was riding round on tall and ancient bike.

He arrived here on it one day, met a friend and went off to lunch with him, quite forgetting the bike standing in Cross Street. Next day he remembered it, came down in flap because there were cycle thieves about, and found old velocipede still safe and sound against the kerb. In gratitude, he pedalled down to the church and went and put half a crown in the offerings box. When he came out, his bike had gone.

To-day, old Gaspin was holding forth to Gudgeon on the pleasures of selling books in Victoria's reign. 'Every customer was a gentleman in those days.' Gudgeon blows out his cheeks and says nothing as usual. 'Ah,' continues Gaspin, growing enthusiastic, 'and they knew a good book when they saw one.'

Here Gudgeon does interrupt – to say that surely this would be a severe handicap to bookseller and publisher alike. Not to be halted by wit, the old man rambles on, while Rexine motions the rest of us to get on with our work. Retiring into background, last sentence of Gaspin's I catch is: 'The book trade isn't what it was.' Now where have I heard that before? The earliest papyrus ever dug up on the site of Ur bears the inscription, 'The book trade isn't what it was.'

Getting dark horribly early these evenings. Went walk with Jack, caught several glimpses of telesitters huddled round their sets. Must be bad times for door-to-door selling of encyclopaedias.

FRIDAY

Pay-day. Something had gone wrong with the organization and our dumb office wench did not lumber round with the envelopes till nearly lunch time. After I've paid laundry bill and settled with Mrs Yell there's precious little cash left; can't think why I stay on at Brightfount's.

It being market day, I went to look at the stalls. Often wish Mr B.

would let me take a barrow of dead stock out to sell off cheap. There was scruffy fellow with trunks full of rubbishy old volumes and people jostling to get a look in. Mrs Humphry Ward and Ouida going like hot cakes.

Busy afternoon, shop packed. One customer barged into another who was squatting to look into Zoology and stood on the tail of his mackintosh, so that when the other straightened up there was an ominous ripping sound. This was the most exciting moment of the day.

SATURDAY
Odd bod in who said he used to run a private press in the thirties. 'Quite a paying game: every title used to be half buckram, limited to fifty copies – we'd print two hundred of each.' Bought nothing of course.

Had to go round to library with a couple of books. Nice girl there, name of Ruth. Fancy we might have more than literary interests in common.

Notice that while Mr B. is away Arch Rexine has taken up several of his little habits. For instance, unlocking the tills at about 4.30 and having a peep to see how much we've taken. Nasty, miserly habit, but somehow Mr B. made it look cosy and reassuring. Rexine's sarcastic comment on seeing me watch him: 'Heaven knows where *your* next week's wages are coming from!'

September

SUNDAY

Was lying on bed reading last chapter of *A Land* and half thinking about walk before lunch, when Mrs Yell burst angrily into room. Quite startled to see look on her face. Slipped shoes quickly off counterpane and asked if anything was wrong.

'You mean to say you can't hear all that shouting and hooting out the front?'

Said not from where I was (the back).

'Well, it's someone after you. You'd better come quick. I should reckon they're drunk, carrying on like that at this time of a Sunday morning.'

Feeling rather annoyed myself, stuck head out of landing window. There was an odd hoot or two coming up – Derek stood by his crock, staring impatiently up. Directly he saw me he told me to come down at once; he and Myra were going to take me out for the day: I was to 'descend suitably equipped for tennis and aquatic sports'.

Could not help feeling surprised that they wanted me for company. Collected my stuff under grim eye of Mrs Yell, who said merely as I hurried out, 'Is that your Uncle's son?'

'Yes.'

'Ha! I *thought* as much.'

Pressed downstairs. Derek stood on pavement; Myra was just

69

climbing out of the car with another girl. 'Hello, sweetest cousin!' she called. 'We've dragged my sister Sheila along to keep you company.'

It was Miranda!

It was the dark, wistful girl who had bought the Ordnance map off me a couple of months ago! Directly they told me her name was Sheila I saw how wonderfully she fitted it and it fitted her. Recognized her in a flash, although she did not recognize me; nor was she looking wistful. She had just begun a choc-ice, which she poked at me in a friendly but formal manner and said, 'Have a bite.'

'Pile in with her, old scout,' said Derek. 'We haven't got all day.'

He added as he climbed into the front with Myra, 'and don't do anything I wouldn't do!'

Roaring with laughter, he pulled off the massive hand brake and we were away.

The day was enjoyable, but only painfully so. We stopped for lunch at whacking great brand-new roadhouse on the A 25, a pseudo-Tudor palace cheerfully labelled 'The Hydrogen Age' with a big mushroom cloud on its sign. Here we had drinks, and Derek stood us all very nice (expensive) meal.

Played tennis there – my first game since Avril left! – but not very successful: had to wait ages for court, and Derek had *no idea*. Then we drove down to quiet but smelly bit of river for bathe; girls managed to change in car, we changed behind bushes and I trod barefoot on some nettles. Myra would not go in, said it looked too filthy. Certainly tasted filthy.

Sheila looked – oh, marvellous in her costume.

On way home she was telling me that she has got little furnished flat with friends in Maidstone, and starts a job there soon. So we shall not be seeing much of her in these parts.

MONDAY
Arrived, as I sometimes do, before nine o'clock. Old Mr Parsons was sweeping shop out with long melancholy strokes.

'Forget anything on Saturday?' he asked.

'No,' I said, and then remembered. Mrs Callow had brought me slice of home-made cherry cake; I took a bite then had to serve and forgot it.

'The cake!' I exclaimed. 'It's been in my drawer all week-end.'

'That's a fact it hasn't,' Mr Parsons said.

Soon found what he meant. The rats, without which no good bookshop is complete, had scoffed every crumb. Unfortunately, the cake had rested on Simpkin's daily order book and half of that was devoured too. Expecting nasty little scene, showed tattered remnant apologetically to Rexine.

He stared at me levelly for about a minute as if in amazement at what he saw and then said quietly, 'I should think your mother was delighted when you decided to leave home, wasn't she?'

Was reminded of the occasion when Edith, cornered in Mr B.'s office with a strawberry wafer, hid it behind a parcel and ruined a nice bit of Sangorski and Sutcliffe binding.

As we were leaving in the evening, Rexine handed me his copy of Langdon-Davies' *The Practice of Bookselling*.

'Try and read this without mutilating it,' he said. 'It's very high-minded: it ought to make you weep.'

TUESDAY

Mr Brightfount returned from holiday. He bought little library on way back yesterday. Good to see him again, seemed pleased to see us. He climbed out of little furniture van, Mrs B. also with him, looking no better or worse for her holiday. She seldom comes in shop, much to our relief. Dave and I helped removals man carry books into one corner, where they rapidly obscured Law and Criminology.

Last object out of the van was a cumbersome object in brown paper. Mr B. took this from me and tried to smuggle it quietly into his office.

'What have you got there, dear?' asked Mrs B. in very female voice.

After a few feeble evasions, the parcel was unwrapped, revealing a gigantic, mounted rhinoceros head. Mr B. explained he had been intending to take it home as a surprise.

'But what on earth should we do with it, Bernard?' his wife asked.

'We could always use it as an ashtray,' he said.

Later, he was so cheerful we told him about the young couple who appeared last week, looking round and leaving without buying anything. 'They wore an aura of suppressed excitement,' Miss Ellis said, doubtless quoting unconsciously from some awful epic.

'I must witness this tantalizing little tableau if they stage it again,' Mr B. said.

'Tantalizing little tableau' . . . That was how I saw it. Admitted diffidently, 'Tried to make up a story out of it the other night in bed – you know, just something short – rather de Maupassanty – but I didn't get far.'

'When you say that, it reminds me of something by Max Beerbohm,' Mr B. said sympathetically. 'Something in *And Even Now*. Hang it, what's that thing called, Archy?'

'I don't know, but I know what you mean,' Rexine said vaguely.

Peeping round, I saw we all looked quite bright. The atmosphere just for a minute was quite literary. Bookselling was what bookselling ideally should be, gentlemanly, fruitful, tender; in my ear sounded Mr Langdon-Davies' voice speaking quietly of 'a lofty function worthily performed'. Even he at that moment might have felt at home among us.

'Well, better get that ruddy rhinoceros out of the way,' Mr B. sighed, breaking the spell.

WEDNESDAY

Ominous card from Folkestone, which simply said: 'We have altered our arrangements and return home to-morrow. Shall be pleased to receive you at "Hatchways" on Sunday as usual.' This rather worried me. There seemed to be so much it refrained from saying.

To cheer me up, Mrs Callow, a motherly type with lemon flavour, suggested one of her 'games'. These we play spasmodically throughout the day; they have bookish associations and speed an odd moment.

Object of to-day's game was to suggest new titles for Hutchinson's handy 'On a Small Income' series.

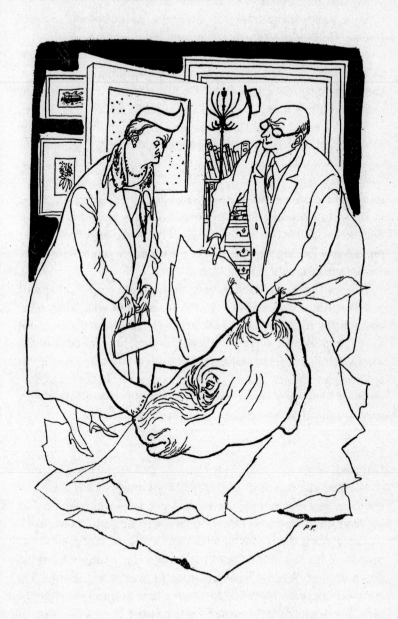

My first one: *Influenza on a Small Income.*

Prize went (unexpectedly) to Gudgeon for *Indigence on a Small Income*. He generally abstains from our childish games.

Momentous news brought in by Mr Parsons as we were closing: he has heard that 'the little bankrupt handbag shop in High Street' (meaning of course that desirable Dodd residence) is being speedily converted into – a bookshop. Opening soon!

'Now's your chance,' Dave tells me. 'If you nip in quick they're probably still wanting a bright lad for errand boy.'

THURSDAY
Rare event: customer waiting on doorstep at nine. Thereafter, people in and out all morning. Sold three copies of *Retire and Enjoy it*. We've done well with that book. Notice most of the buyers have been young, presumably looking well ahead. 'It's the twentieth century answer to *De Senectute*,' one of them told me.

Dropped book into Public Library during lunch hour. V. charming girl there; Ruth: dark brown hair, etc. Managed to get talking to her and actually had the cheek to ask her out. Unfortunately she is one of the 'two nights a week handicrafts, two nights a week dramatic society' kind, but finally talked her into next Monday evening. As soon as I got outside again I regretted asking her; in the heat of the moment I had quite forgotten about Sheila. But after all she's miles away – and certainly without a thought to spare for me.

FRIDAY
Got paid.

Worked like dog most of day, Edith grumpily assisting some of the time, throwing out old correspondence and invoices more than six years old. These were housed under deep dust up in rear attic.

Came down about four to wash hands, saw old Gudgeon sitting placidly at his seat in the Topog. room. Wonder whatever he thinks about all day? When I went up again he was sitting reading *The Bookseller*, apparently waiting for closing time as we all do, although generally in more tactful ways, Rexine's nature being what it is.

The Bookseller is our trade paper, appears every Saturday, and records events in the world of books; famous publishers at parties, amateur theatricals at W.H. Smith's, or new bookshops in Portsmouth, all get their pictures in *The Bookseller*. Am proud to say that even Brightfount's has been mentioned in it.

SATURDAY

Was re-dressing side window and staring rather blankly into Bottomley Place when Peggy Ellis nudged me. 'They're here again,' she whispered.

'Who?'

'Your Maupassant ending.'

She was right. The strange couple were floating quietly round the shop with dreamy eyes and occasional affectionate glances at each other. They watched with some interest while Dave served a customer with typing paper. When Mr B. emerged from his office, they looked suddenly guilty and made to go. As they reached the door, old customer, A. H. Markham, was coming in.

'Ah, Reggy and Babs!' he exclaimed, seizing their arms and smiling wider than we've ever seen him smile. 'Fancy finding you *here*, of all places. I must introduce you at once to my good friend Bernard Brightfount.'

And so I got my Maupassant ending. Markham's acquaintances were newlyweds; they had been stealing a preview of bookshop routine (in *Brightfount's*!) before opening on their new pitch in High Street.

Espionage on a small income?

SUNDAY

Autumnal nip in the air. Summer slips away so quickly. As I turned up Uncle's drive, I could see him in the vegetable garden, digging up carrots or something. He was puffing so industriously I got quite close before he looked up. He had a black eye!

Instantly pictured all sorts of ghastly scenes at Folkestone hotel – indignant lady guest assaulting Uncle, or Uncle assaulting head waiter.

'It's all right,' he said, seeing my startled look. 'Just had a bit of an accident, that's all. Just got to get these carrots up and then we'll go on in and have a sherry.'

He seemed in good form, which was something more than could be said for Aunt Anne when we got indoors. She sat rather glumly while Uncle rattled on about the sea breezes and a cinemascope cowboy film someone at the hotel had taken them to – first time he has been inside a cinema for years.

'But what happened to your eye?' I asked.

'I must get on with lunch, or it'll never be ready by the time Derek and Myra get back,' Aunt interposed, hurrying out.

'My eyes have been bothering me lately,' Uncle began. 'I don't see so well as I used to, get a lot of stabbing pains. So I've taken to shutting them whenever I can, to give them a rest. I often walk about here with them closed, but of course *here* I'm used to the territory. At the hotel I wasn't. I suppose I should have been more careful, but you don't think till these things have happened. Anyhow, this night I went up alone to the bedroom, never even bothered to put the light on and walked smack into the wardrobe.'

Told him how sorry I was. He leant closer and said, 'It's nothing, Peter, nothing to worry about at all. The only trouble is the *fuss* Anne made about the whole thing, insisted we came home and everything. Now is it reasonable?'

Said lamely I expected she was worried about his health.

'You won't understand,' he said dolefully. 'You're a shallow, happy creature – and I wouldn't have you otherwise for a moment, but you don't know how *complicated* life can be.'

Was both amused and offended, but merely said hoped his eye would be soon be better.

When Derek and Myra arrived there was no time for consecutive thought. He has now got a job in London with a firm he once worked for in Singapore. And Sheila is quite happy in her new job!

MONDAY
Beastly wet morning. Various bitter comments on horrors of English climate from staff who have some distance to come to work. Mr

Parsons: 'Worse than the summer, isn't it?' Arch Rexine, who got soaked on his motor bike ride here: 'I'm thinking of writing my autobiography with the title *Forty Years Under Water*.'

Good pile of catalogue orders to get on with. Long one from fellow in New Zealand who did not give item numbers. His letter slipped to bottom of pile – mild punishment for exasperating habit! You classify the books, you arrange them in alphabetical order, you number them: you might just as well not bother.

As rain petered off, customers began to appear; first businesslike ones with dripping umbrellas, then browsers with slightly damp macs, and then casuals with no macs at all. So we get hints of the Great Outdoors indoors.

Many casuals seem scared to come in. The Penguins near the door do the trick, and next to them we keep the 'Teach Yourself' section. Odd how those two blocks of books have jackets familiar and reassuring to the Great British Public – and without all the advertisement employed by those two potent beverages, Horlicks and Guinness.

Out in the evening with Ruth from public library. Conversation was not solely of books. (As a matter of fact, it was mostly about her dramatic society; will get roped in for that if not careful.)

Saw her to her house; she would insist on my going in. Father quite formidable old boy with walrus moustache. He began talking about someone he knew and evidently expected me to know. 'Mind you, he's a complete ignoramus,' he said, '– never read a book with footnotes in his life!'

TUESDAY
Rev. Mullion in. Dear man! So vague, yet so persistent. For over a year now we've been trying to get him an out of print pamphlet published for 1s. 6d. back in 1923. He just popped in to-day (the popping occupying half an hour) to tell us he would really like *two* copies if we could manage it. Blessed are they that have faith in the Book Trade!

Trouble after lunch! The surly carpenter Vaws and his mate are still at work re-shelving the Slaughterhouse. Last week they never appeared at all. To-day poor old Mr Parsons was complaining because they trod mud on to his polished floors.

'That bloke Vaws don't work when he *is* here!' he commented. Vaws heard, and a good 'earty argument ensued. Mr Brightfount had to part them, and they both went grumpily back to work.

The shop was pretty full of customers.

The carpenter, in righteous wrath, seized a plank rather wildly and put it (accidentally) through the Slaughterhouse window. Tinkling and clattering distinctly heard in shop, followed by ominous hush. 'What was that?' someone asked.

'That,' said Mrs Callow calmly, 'Was a vaze, varze or Vaws.'

WEDNESDAY

Witty remark from Gudgeon. Customer looking dubiously at the Van Nostrand *Scientific Encyclopaedia* we had ordered for him. 'I wonder if it is quite what I wanted!' he says, glancing nervously at price.

'Of course reference books are like wives,' says Gudgeon agreeably. 'It's only when you've taken them home and lived with them a bit that you really find out what they are like.'

As Mrs Callow says, from a confirmed bachelor this is not merely good, it's visionary.

Half-day. Aunt Doris came over and we had pleasant afternoon, visited museum, tea at the Odalisque (she paid). In usual fashion, she only decided to come this morning, sent me typical telegram: MEET ME STATION 2.15 THIS AFTERNOON FULL STOP AUNT DORIS.

THURSDAY

Minor panic because Edith, our dumb office wench, forgot to type out *Clique* list until almost too late. I say 'minor' because she forgets every week, and we are all hardened to it by now – except her.

All of morning's customers seemed to want difficult books which we had not got. Most of the titles I had never heard of – some of them Arch Rexine hadn't either, I'm *sure*; but he bluffs well and so you can't tell: and he's not the sort you dare ask . . .

Am always awed by confident men who ask airily for Beach's little pamphlet, *On the use of 'One' as a Prop-word*, or MacMillipenny *On the Judiciary Courts of the General Eyre prior to the Bandage Act of 1475*. I hurry away to appropriate corner of shop muttering title, and spend undue time gazing at gap on shelves in case am accused of not looking properly.

Confidence, shattered easily by this kind of thing, restored shortly before closing. Large lady in duffle coat and much rouge entered.

'Have you got a second-hand copy of *Les Misérables*?' she asked.

'I should think so, madam. Do you want a translation?'

'Oh no,' she said firmly. 'It must be in English.'

FRIDAY

Pay-day.

Now have three definite orders for Charles Chilton's *Journey into Space*. Gudgeon claims that science-fiction is not quite Brightfount's style. Dave says it should be; we must keep up-to-date, etc., and adds crushingly, 'Anyhow, didn't we have to order Prebendary Courtnay a copy of *The Complete Book of Outer Space*?'

Gudgeon (with splendid irrelevancy): 'Tell me, where is Inner, or where are Out and Outest Space?'

SATURDAY

V. busy to-day. Catalogue orders up to expectation. Best stuff going overseas, westwards. Also piles of books to sort away. They nearly barricade Mr B. into his office; he dumps them stack by stack outside his door as he has marked them. Lot of rubbish to be pulped, books and dust jackets. Retrieved broken copy of *Hand of Ethelberta* to read.

Got back to digs to find letter awaiting me. At least, it had been put by my plate as usual, but as I went into the living-room Gyp was jumping down off my chair and carting letter over to mat. Mr Yell was out at the back, Mrs Yell charged in and retrieved letter before any damage was done.

Have never seen anything so ludicrously wicked and furtive as look on dog's face! If he were human, you'd think for sure he was repenting one murder and planning another.

Letter was brief – from Avril! Half pleasant, entirely noncommittal: hardly know why she wrote it.

It scarcely hurt at all.

Sunday

Very savage.

Was in two minds whether to go over to Uncle's or not, but decided they would probably be expecting me. Pretty poor morning, so waited and caught the 12.15 bus to Wickham Princes, which put me off at Graves turn and left me only about a mile to walk.

Got there, found a note from Derek pinned on back door.

'Father has unwisely mentioned a house he saw for sale over in Hythe which sounds absolutely our cup of char so we're flogging up the old war horses and going out to view. Help yourself to windfalls, armchair, gin (in mod.) or slice off raw joint.

Be good.

Love.'

Could just visualize, between lines of this not very funny epistle, Uncle and Aunt being egged on to do the eighty-odd mile journey. Whatever Derek wants to live there for, can't imagine – much too far to get to London from every day.

Monday

Had slight twinge of that Monday morning feeling. Perhaps it was the sight of those old familiar titles as I slip in side door. Permanent guests: *An Insufficiency of Roses*, *Soft Thoughts for Hard Heads*, *Shouting Down a Cliff*, *The Mud Yield*. They've lodged too long at Brightfount's. Probably we shall never sell them: if someone doesn't steel them, we shall have to steel ourselves to throw them out.

But after all, there may not be copies of those four partic. books in any other bookshop in England. Somebody might advertise for them in *Clique* one day; one day, somebody might even come in and *ask* for them . . .

No, I admit it doesn't sound likely.

Funny how after a time you forget why you bought the books in the first place. We have several new books like that. Arch Rexine almost growls when he passes those three shaggy copies of *Withdrawn Game* that he ordered off Malpractice and Stimms just before they went bust. Suppose *Withdrawn Game* was one of the reasons *why* they went bust.

Gave Rexine back his *Practice of Bookselling*. Thanked him, said had found it interesting.

Rexine: 'Huh! I wish I'd got a *Practice of Carpentering* to lend that man Vaws.' Latter has not turned up again to-day.

TUESDAY

Landlady Mrs Yell tackled me gently on landing as I was coming to work. 'I don't want to nag, dear,' she said, 'But if you could just give your jacket a brush down before you leave work, it would save an awful lot of work. Nobody *knows* how much fluff I get from under your bed, and in me heart of hearts I'm sure it comes from that bookshop.'

She's one of those simple women with a love of shiny surfaces: forever polishing. Sometimes wonder how poor old Mr Yell and Gyp put up with it.

Peggy Ellis not at work. She had a slight sniffle yesterday, accentuated as much as possible by constant plying of a handkerchief. Her Mum came in during morning, confided in Mr B. that Peggy was riddled with cold.

Business, nevertheless, as usual.

New bookshop in High Street opens next week – Reggie and Babs must be busy behind scenes. They'll be in time to catch the Christmas trade. Certain amount of furtive interest displayed in the affair here. Only comment heard from Mr B. was the mild and defensive, 'Well, this is a fair-sized cathedral town; there should be room for two good bookshops.'

81

As usual, Rexine was slightly more sarcastic. 'This will be a challenge to us,' he told Dave and me, 'A challenge which will be met by the employers with a new coat of paint on the outside of the shop, and by the employees' – he gazed at the two of us in mock-despair – 'by ceasing to sit and sharpen pencils on to the floor with bowie knives while serving customers.'

Dave managed to look fairly innocent.

Book humping up and down stairs most of afternoon, felt glad to get home and sit down. Postcard from Aunt Anne, view of Hythe, posted in Hythe, saying: 'Nasty day here, sea quite rough. Sorry we had to make early start. Trouble with inside of Derek's car delayed us an hour on the way'.

Poor Aunt!

WEDNESDAY
More book-lugging. From Mr B.'s office to lower shop, from cellar to attic, from upstairs to Slaughterhouse, from attic to cellar. Carried *Journal of Royal Agriculture Society of Scotland*, Vols. XXXIV to LXXXVI (lacks XLI–XLIV), to above Topog. by mistake. Mr B.: 'Never mind, leave it where it is now; you've cleared a good bit of space which may come in useful.' He stood and gazed at the gap, which was in cellar. Fear he may get ideas about clearing out down there.

Time has stood still down in our cellar. Where to start would be the big puzzle – almost as big a puzzle as what happened to Vols. XLI–XLIV.

Half-day. Went long walk over Baggar's Dune way with Mr Callow, back to tea with them. Mrs C. very good cook. Overate. V. cheerful evening: friends of theirs, the Mollimores, in; got back to digs guiltily after 11 p.m. All quiet and dark at 61 – usual niff of Lifebuoy and damp cookery.

THURSDAY
Peggy Ellis back. Sweet little thing really. Bit useless, all the same.

Trying to sort out query, was digging in file and found in

WAR–WIZ garish little rag entitled *Showdown Showgirl*. Intriguing advert on back: 'Men! Are You Embarrassed By Insufficient Superfluous Hair? Grow a Real He-Man Crop My Way. Ten Day Trial or MONEY BACK. Luxuriant Growth Guaranteed.'

Edith, our dumb office wench, passed. 'Hey, that's mine!' she said, and grabbed it.

Occupied most of morning fiddling about, getting nothing done. Coincidence: Mrs Callow sold a copy of *Withdrawn Game* funny I should have mentioned it. Who on earth would have wanted six famous sportsmen's views on the Afterlife? Sometimes try when I come in morning to guess what books will go during day; never guess right. Our selection's too large, our customers too peculiar.

Mr Parsons at 2.30: 'Here, look sharp, Mr B. wants you in the cellar!'

'What for?'

'Sack, I expect.'

Not quite so bad as that, fortunately – although as Dave says, I could always have a shot at asking Reggie and Babs for a job! Boss announces firmly he wants Dave and me to start turning out end of cellar first thing to-morrow.

FRIDAY

Pay-day. Started end of cellar. This is actually section we call the Tearoom, because it has gas-ring, bench and heavy bookshelves which cut off rest of cellar. These shelves yielded several interesting mementoes. Old spoutless teapot, old straw hat belonging to Miss Harpe who left last spring, old catalogues, framed photo of Brightfount's with a tram outside it. Cardboard box with mice-nibbled tickets. A 1950 calendar from our wrapping paper people, with hearty Dickensian men round laden table posing for hearty picture entitled 'A Right Royal Repast'.

Worked happily, Dave wearing Miss Harpe's hat, in cloud of dust. Most interesting discovery was following odd little epitaph on flyleaf of 1930 AA book:

On a Defunct Bookseller

So much dead stock! And now his store,
Emptied of books, speaks volumes more:
Death looks him over who was overlooked—
His books are sold, his soul is booked.

Gave this later to Gudgeon, who is odd chap, has morbid streak in him. He read it, nodded without speaking, tore it out of book and tucked it away in an inner pocket. Dave offered him Miss Harpe's hat, but this was refused.

Some progress by end of day. Much dirt swallowed. Last discovery: page from old pre-war comic, *Chatterbox*, featuring Starry Knight, Star of the Circus. Something about these relics rather pathetic, to say nothing of unhygienic!

SATURDAY

New bookshop advertising in local paper. Opening Friday next with speech by local librarian, signing of books and other hoo-ha. Special visit from famous lady novelist. Rexine's promised painters began outside this morning: their ladders against the window give us besieged feeling – and with Vaws we also have the enemy within the gates. He's nearly finished, praise be. He turned up yesterday, without apology.

Astonished to see Mr Yell enter shop looking sheepish and furtive. 'Is anything wrong?' I asked. 'Is the house on fire?'

'I'm ever so sorry to come barging in here like this,' he said, ignoring my question; 'I've got a book to sell you.' From under his coat he produced, wrapped in newspaper, a copy of *The Cruel Sea*.

'But it's the copy someone gave you for a present last Christmas,' I said.

'Yes, I know, but you see I just finished it this week, and Vera don't like books lying about making the place untidy if they aren't actually being used.'

Mr B. said he supposed it was worth four bob to us. I told this to Mr Yell, who accepted it, still looking staggered to find himself in a bookshop.

'I shouldn't have come in like this,' he said. 'Only Vera happened to look inside it and see one of the shore-leave bits, and she made me bring it up here straight away. You know what she is.'

Quite hectic afternoon up to about 4.30, then slack. Gudgeon abruptly said to Mrs Callow, 'You like playing games. How about composing an up-to-date epigram on a defunct bookseller?' After humming and haaing till time to go home, she produced following on Distant Prospect of a Bookseller's Hearse:

> *Farewell old friend! Slowly you take, I see,*
> *This one last journey order carriage free.*

September–October

SUNDAY

'Hello! I had a letter from little sister Sheila yesterday,' was Myra's greeting to me, 'and she sent you her love.'

Muttered something inadequate, wondering at the same time if Sheila really *had*.

'Haven't you got any nice little girl friends of your own age here?'

Said positively No, detested women.

'Ah, you disillusionized old roué! Come and sit by Momma Myra's side and tell her all about it – at least till that jealous oaf of a husband of mine appears.

'You know, I *distinctly* recall the first time I was really in love. Oh, it was truly romantic – boring, really, but romantic. He was so young. *I* was so young . . . Calf-love, of course. And the funny thing was my infatuation for him was in no way dimmed by the fact that I could quite clearly see how ridiculous he was.

'Coming blackberrying with us this afternoon? Everywhere should be soaking after last night's rain.'

Asked her about the house at Hythe. Only answer I got was, 'My dear, don't mention the house at Hythe. Derek was absolutely *furious*!'

Derek, however, seemed perfectly mild. Gave me long technical explanation over lunch why his car broke down. Something to do with a fan belt.

Blackberried in afternoon, Aunt and Uncle plodding cheerfully along with us in gum-boots. Feeling rather mean, avoided Aunt as much as poss., but at one point she got me alone behind the others and hissed, 'Did your Uncle ever tell you why we had to leave the Folkestone hotel? – it was because he locked himself in the W.C. all one day.'

She is obviously under emotional stress; never under ordinary circumstances would she bring herself to mention a W.C. to a younger relative.

'But his eye—' I began.

'And then there was this silly, embarrassing business about changing his name. Your Uncle signed himself Aldys all the time we were there. Naturally, I've never breathed a word about it to the rest of the family; what they'd say I don't know. And when I had a letter from your poor Aunt Doris addressed to me in the usual way . . . well, I was very upset, I don't mind telling you. The waiter at our table saw it and I'm sure he suspected there was an ambiguous relationship between your Uncle and I – me.'

'But Uncle's eye—'

'Oh, his eye! He invented a very strange story to cover that, but I have my own ideas as to how he – yes, we're just coming, Derek. There's a whole *bough* full of nice big ones here.'

Uncle always seems fairly ordinary to me. Wonder if perhaps poor Aunt is not right when she suggests he may deliberately be attempting to be odd, and he confines most of it to an audience of one. But should certainly like to know how he did get that black eye – which is only faint shore-sea green to-day.

MONDAY

Chestnut trees in cathedral close are a heavenly colour – caught a glimpse of them through Aeffing's Gate on way to work. Painters already doing front of shop when I got there. Stood and chatted to one of them before going inside where the delish. cool air never penetrates.

Dreamy morning. Left alone in shop most of time. Sad little

publisher's representative drifted in and went upstairs to see Mr Brightfount.

Travellers often seem prosaic men. They wear their responsibilities lightly. But I always have a feeling of great things stirring when I see one of them sit down next to Mr B. and open up his little case. Out of it, he draws a catalogue containing titles of and information on books due to see daylight in the next four or six months: books as yet not books, hopes, schedules, pulp and typescript merely, something which the public may acclaim but of which it as yet knows nothing, another Tennyson in bud, a new Orwell flowering. The bookseller nods and turns to the next item.

'You shouldn't miss that one, you know,' says the traveller, disinterested but anxious.

'Oh, why's that?' Mr B. asks.

'It's *the* book on Soviet brain-washing systems.'

'I've got no customers interested in that.'

'Written by an expert, Manuel Laybor, who has himself personally been brain-washed half-a-dozen times. It's *bound* to sell.'

'Not here,' says Mr B. firmly.

'Even here,' says the traveller with equal firmness. 'Of course, I don't want to press it, but I've heard on the q.t. from Sir Bruce that it's very likely to be chosen by *Junior Lilliput* as their Book of the Year. Take a couple of copies and see how it goes.'

TUESDAY
We had just opened – Mr Parsons was brushing down the front with air of a man sweeping gravestones, I was arranging shilling books on their stand in the porch – when Ruth appeared.

'I thought you must be ill as I hadn't seen you for so long,' she says. Amazing how some women are totally incapable of drawing correct conclusions.

My trouble is am too easy-going. Weakly told her I'd been busy and would meet her in evening – from which session have just returned! Ruth was twenty minutes late. Told me *ad lib.* about her handicraft lessons – could almost make raffia mats myself by time she had finished. Only other topic, her dramatic club . . . This can't go on.

Finished yesterday's cat. orders by tea break, started on today's. Sold our nice copy of *Woodward's Ecclesiastical Heraldry*; Gudgeon said Thomas Thorp had a copy recently, but he wasn't asking as much for it as we were for ours.

Certain excitement about new bookshop opening on Friday. Several customers have asked us what we think about it. It'll be more central than we are, but no corner site and not so big. Looks rather chromium and marble, more like butcher than bookseller, and name rather ostentatious over door.

'What are the rivals called?' asked Mrs Callow when new façade was first revealed.

'Pardon's,' Dave told her.

'I see,' said Mrs C., grinning pleasantly at this gift of a chance to pun. 'Pardon, eh? . . . a sorry name.'

According to Ruth, Reggie Pardon has been scrounging round the library for orders already. And I suppose he's got Avril's old bedroom crammed full of thrillers and d'oyley sets.

WEDNESDAY

Half-day. Before we had closed, painters had finished outside, and the legend: BOOKS B. BRIGHTFOUNT & CO. PRINTS stood out neatly off-white on black.

Vaws, too, has nearly finished. He's really not half as bad as he looks; trouble is, that squint eye gives him villainous appearance.

Don't know what he can have heard me saying about Mrs Yell, but he told me this morning, 'If you feel like chucking up your digs and trying somewhere else any time, my son and his wife have just moved into a house of their own down Poultney Street, number 5, Skegness Villas, and I expect they'd be glad to have a quiet young boarder in.'

Thanked him for his kind offer but said I would stick it out at 61 North Terrace.

Football in afternoon: first game of season, may be last. Piggy

Dexter talked me into it, lent me boots, which didn't fit. Inside right. Played on Bagger's Lane field, game interrupted by stray pig on pitch.

Mrs Yell seemed sorry for me, 'all that dirty mud on your knees', as she expressed it, gave me fish and chips for supper and made me sit by their great coal fire instead of my small, popping gas one upstairs, and listen to their radio. Why are people on Wilfred Pickles' programme always so keen to sing 'Lily of Laguna'?

THURSDAY
Slept like log and was stiff this morning.

Copy of *The Bankrupt Bookseller* turned up in shop. Quite interesting to dip into, although on the whole depressing – like that other fictitious bookseller in Arnold Bennett's *Riceyman Steps*.

Bankrupt Bookseller said he would rather sell cookery book than novel. Had same feeling myself when Dave sold most exotic character our solitary copy of *Dishes from the Southern Hemisphere*. Character had been everywhere, seen everywhere, eaten everything, including blind white fish in Persia during war; later on he travelled right up river Amazon with rubber firm – showed Dave photo of himself in jungle clearing, frying python, which he claimed tasted like frogs' legs. Also claimed to have eaten bat pie; didn't say what that tasted like. V. interesting, but missed half of it myself serving dreary man fussing over Le Blond print of Brighton.

Red letter day! Slaughterhouse re-decorations at last finished. Vaws, truculent, and very much in charge of ops., took Mr B. and Rexine in with due ceremony and said, 'There you are. Looks too good for books, doesn't it?'

As he was helping his junior to pack up, old Mr Parsons, who for weeks has been waging anti-Vaws campaign, remarked, 'So you're going at last then, mate! I thought we was saddled with you for good.'

'Oh, saddled, were you?' says Vaws sourly. 'If you were saddled there's nobody alive could tell you from Foxhunter's grandfather.' And with that he goes.

Woke with the feeling something odd was on: Pardon's grand opening! Seems funny to think of sentimental associations I have with that place.

Made poor start. Dropped shaving brush out of open bathroom window, went downstairs, hunted unsuccessfully in yard among pile of logs, between few slug-chewed Michaelmas daisies and behind Gyp's kennel. Mr Yell wouldn't lend his: it was 'unhealthy' he said. So to work late and unshaven.

'How truly typical,' sighed Arch Rexine when he heard the sad story. 'The day we're supposed to be on our toes, you don't know if you're on your head or your heels.'

By all accounts, the opening of Pardon's was quite a successful affair. A loudspeaker van toured round town inviting everyone in friendly and well-modulated tones to attend the opening at 10.45 a.m. City Librarian made little speech, opened shop, presumably in name of Culture. Local reporter took photos. Wing-Commander Digby Foible, D.S.O., imported for occasion, signed copies of his best-selling war book, *Power Dive over Pontestura*, which neatly combines dam-damaging with P.O.W. appeal. He shook hands agreeably with everyone and had his fountain pen pinched before morning was over.

In afternoon, one of our most promising lady novelists, Olivia Bedworth, drove down and gaily gave away signed photos of herself in period dress to anyone who bought her period novel, *Not To-night, Lord Leicester*, price 9s. 6d. Whether she was late for the opening or specially designed to appeal to afternoon shoppers, we do not know. Apparently she *did* appeal to the shoppers – and to Wing-Commander Foible, who stayed to keep a friendly eye on her.

Grapevine (in the shape of one of Mr Parsons' many little nieces) reported brisk sales there, and several dozen copies of *Not To-night, Lord Leicester* were purchased. Perhaps event had made public book-minded, because throughout the day our sales also were – that seems to be the word to use – brisk. We even shifted a copy of Miss Bedworth's previous book, *This Supple Blade*!

After an early tea, the Wing Co. and the lady novelist drove happily back to London together in the former's car.

SATURDAY

Trouble with Mrs Yell. Apparently I had 'been and trod down' all her best Micks yesterday. New shaving brush was v. bristly and breakfast toast was burnt. Thinking of getting married. But to whom?

Dear old Mr Gaspin, who once owned Brightfount's, put in an appearance. Must be ninety and has hat to match.

'Well, Mr Gaspin,' says Gudgeon, 'did you attend the opening of our new rivals yesterday?'

'Yes,' Mr G. confesses, 'I did; the spectacle of literature rampant in the High Street proved irresistible! But you must remember this. Pardon is not your rival, whatever you may think. He's in the same great battle you are, the Crusade against Illiteracy.'

No TV to-night, Lord Leicester?

October

Determined to tackle someone about Uncle Leo.

Derek was in the garage polishing up his car. Told him I was getting upset about his father.

'Not to worry, old boy,' he said. 'I don't.'

'This is serious, Derek. You'd think so, too, if you'd seen him standing in the middle of the fishpond with his shoes and socks on.'

At this he does show mild interest. 'When was this?' he asks.

'This summer.'

'Crikey, Peter, I thought you meant *now!* Wouldn't have missed it for worlds. What was he doing it for – cooling off?'

Said in constricted voice that Uncle had been thinking of putting tessellation on rear parapet. Whereupon Derek comes solemnly round bonnet and asks, 'And did you think it was a good idea?'

Challenged him to say this was not odd behaviour.

'No, not for Father. Actually he did mention this tessellation stunt to me. I told him to go ahead with it. Pep the old place up a bit – you must admit yourself it's a damn ordinary-looking house.'

Abandoned this line of approach and asked how Uncle got his black eye.

Derek puts fatherly arm on my shoulder and says, 'Alas, Peter, me old son, you've lived too long in the cloistered atmosphere of

93

that bookshop. You've no idea of the passions that motivate ordinary human beings! I expect Father made a pass at a curvaceous barmaid when Mother wasn't looking and got a back-hander for his trouble.'

Gave up *pro tem* but returned to attack after lunch, when we were all having coffee, by asking Uncle himself about the tessellation.

'Oh, I shan't proceed any further with that idea. I'm getting too much of an old man to bother about appearances any more. Besides, we may be selling up the house soon and then where's the point?'

Aunt looks up sharply as if to say that it is the first she has heard about selling up, and Myra slides on to the carpet and grips his knees, exclaiming, 'Leo, dearest – selling up! How wildly exciting you make it sound! *Do* tell us you're a secret gambler and unknown to us have been up to your neck in debt for years and suddenly—'

'Nothing like that at all!'

'How *dis*appointing. Couldn't you just picture us all sitting round on boxes while the broker's men carted all the stuff away.'

'I only mentioned selling up, Myra, because I was thinking of that house in Hythe you and Derek didn't like. I'm sure I could knock 'em down to three thousand for it.'

'That ghastly place! My dear, they'd creosoted the lavatory seat!'

'I dare say that could be remedied.'

MONDAY

What Mr Gaspin calls Pardon's 'Crusade against Illiteracy' has begun with a window full of jigsaw puzzles, packs of cards, wedding cake decorations, cruet sets bearing the arms of the town and a neat handwritten notice, 'You are cordially invited to buy your Christmas cards here'.

Our junior partner sporadically keeps what he calls a Blurb Album, 1,001 Gems of the Puff-Writer's Art. Found a prize for him, first thing: Sheridan Le Fanu's prose described as being of a 'deliciously clear, unfusty style that diffuses a pale amber, melancholy light like bog-water'. This from a second-hand omnibus.

Rexine was copying this into album, when Peggy Ellis poked head round door and said, 'There's a parson outside wants a Sarum missile. If we had one, would it be in Military?'

'I'll go,' says Rexine tersely. Returns in a moment and says, 'It was in Theology, it was two vols., it was a Missal not a missile, and that parson happened to be the Bishop.'

As Peggy explained after, she wasn't feeling too good, and bishop or not he spoke with a plum in his mouth. After lunch she didn't come back!

Somewhat niggling day. Edith, our dumb office wench, unhappy because new till was 1s. 4d. down on Saturday. Gudgeon, industriously cataloguing upstairs, put his pen down somewhere and spent half-hour looking for it. Mr Brightfount and Mrs Callow were just starting some complicated business with the catalogue cards, which need revising, when a supply of stationery arrived; everything dropped while Purchase Tax is wrestled with.

Another duty never done: pile of prospectuses for Wilfrid Noyce's *South Col* which we wrote for and then somehow never sent out. Now they'll lie in the cellar until Everest is built all over with semi-detacheds! If you sent out all the prospectuses the publishers present you with, it would cost you a fortune in postage and labour.

TUESDAY

Peggy Ellis's Mum swept in and was ushered before Rexine, whom she informed that her daughter was indisposed with a cold in her abdomen. Dave, who generally overhears such things, overheard this things. He regaled us with the old joke about the army private who reported sick with a pain in his abdomen, whereupon the orderly corporal answers, 'Only officers have abdomens, sergeants have stomachs, and yours is a —— belly.'

Poor old Mrs Yell is also under weather, which has been foul yesterday and to-day, raining without cease. She emerged at breakfast time with shocking cold.

'I feel like a washed-out rag,' she admitted gloomily. 'But I know it's no good me doing anything about it. If I gets one now it's on me till Sexagesima, on and off. I'll get some of them paper hankies when I'm out shopping.'

There's an old book out in the shilling shelves which catches my eye whenever I pass. Dull green, grimy, worn, it's been there a long time. On the spine are the words, BALLET. BRASSICA CROPS. Really must look into it sometime and see whether it's a book by a Mr Ballet on Brassica Crops, or a book on ballet by a Miss Brassica Crops.

Local drama critic, Ralph Mortlake, in. Wanted to have back book he sold us some weeks ago, review copy. Rather awkward as it was in with new stock. He was in splendid humour with himself, did v. funny parody of recent political speech he had heard — orotund voice declaring, 'And I think we all feel in a very real sense what a very real sense of values we have had, ah, adumbrated here this evening, and in particular how very, very ably they have been, ah, adumbrated. It therefore gives me very real pleasure . . .' etc.

Wish I could get him interested in Ruth. Or her in him. Have nasty feeling she is about to appear again.

WEDNESDAY

Nipped out in tea break and put old brown jacket in Achille Serre's to be cleaned. Back to find Sir Roger Wynd in shop. Was glad I had suit on, especially as Lady Wynd also was there, tall figure in purple dress with hair to match. Together, they create a ghastly sense of occasion in our homely surroundings. Staff all terrified of Sir Roger, except Mr B. who handles him expertly.

Sir Roger is formidably knowledgeable and wears his scholarship darkly – or heavily, whichever is opposite of wearing it lightly. He wrote *Monkeyspeckle: Essays on the General Decline* in the late twenties, and has since become famous by his silences.

In Brightfount's he talks much too loudly. Had to nip and fetch him an edition of Taylor the Water Poet which Mr B. had reported to him. 'By the way, Brightfount,' he was saying, 'you should read Wittgenstein's *Tractatus Logico-Philosophicus* – or have you?'

'No,' confesses Mr B., 'and that's an understatement.'

Brief literary talk for edification of other customers before Sir

Roger signs cheques and departs. Lady Thelma has not uttered a word since she came in.

Somewhere over our lowly heads, like thunder clouds over a plain, floats the World of Letters. Generally we are unconscious of it; then a few angry drops of rain cause us to look up, and there overhead, gods of the storm, ride the Great Names of literature and their attendant spirits, critics tragical-historical, analytical-tragical and historical-tragical-analytical. Shaken, we dodge behind the nearest best-seller.

Half-day. Out with Ruth in afternoon. She caught me neatly, just as we were coming out of the shop, and invited me to go round to hers about three.

When I got there, she had the sauce to say, 'Our dramatic group is getting so busy now, that really you're lucky I could manage this afternoon.' Not too sure of this. Had to spend most of time rehearsing her in her part in the play: Tweeny in Barrie's *Admirable Crichton*. Must say she's well cast. I had to sit in chair with script while she waltzed round room doing her bit — to delight of her mother, who insisted on remaining with us.

THURSDAY
Nothing happened. Daily round and common cataloguing.

FRIDAY
Pay-day, thank goodness. Owed Mrs Yell 10/- (she was polishing the hall lino at 7.30 this morning, cold or no cold).

Badly written letter from someone in East Hoatley saying we had sent book she had not ordered, should she return it as it was not suitable. Her 'u's', 'n's' and 'r's' all looked exactly the same, consequently it took us some time to work out that the thing in her address which looked like 'uuuueuy' was meant to be 'nunnery'.

Nobody remembered her original letter: nobody ever does! Mr B. got me to dig in the files, finally dicovered she had asked for something by Bunyan and Dave had sent her the new Runyon. Bet that caused a flutter in the uuuueuy!

SATURDAY

Mr B. got me checking over people on our catalogue list. Some haven't ordered for years, and must be removed. Some cards are ages old, with name and adds. written by old Mr Gaspin, and belong to people who order stuff from us year after year; those little cards, with details of how much they ordered, are almost like life histories.

Should love to travel round country meeting these people whom we never see. Miss Rosemary Beacon, of 6 Ankle Lane, Market Harborough, for instance. She's been ordering since 1929. Can just picture her as little old lady in lace cap, sitting by fire and saying to me, 'No, young man, I've never married, but I've led a full life. In fact, I've lived for your catalogues. I can't tell you what a lot of quiet happiness they've brought me throughout the years. Each time I hear the postman in No. 5 I jump up and go to the window—'

'Could you come and serve?' Dave calls up the stairs. 'We've got a shop full of people.'

SUNDAY

Had a head wind against me all the way to Graves St Giles. Directly I got there and saw Aunt's face, I knew something was wrong.

'It's your Uncle,' she said. 'Oh, Peter, he tried to do away with himself. We've had such *trouble* here – I hardly feel I dare leave him a minute.'

She begins to weep, I comfort her as well as I can, and bit by bit the story comes out – her story, anyhow. Apparently Uncle Leo got up on to the roof on Friday morning. Derek, of course was up in London, Myra was out, Aunt was down in the kitchen. He climbed out on to the ridge of the roof and was going to throw himself over the side, down into the yard, but there was a lot of wind about and he slipped. He rolled down the tiles and fell against the parapet, which stopped him going any further.

Colonel Howells and his odd-job man had to come round with a long ladder and rope to get him down. When Uncle was finally safe again, he was suffering from shock and a broken wrist. Aunt was still keeping him in bed.

'Can I go up and see him?' I asked.

'He's down in the study. He would insist on having a campbed in there, because he said it would save my going up and down stairs. Now you must be very careful what you say to him. Don't, whatever you do, excite him. You'll understand he has his his own version of events, which we are pretending to believe.'

This sounded suspish. to me. Went in to see him with some misgivings, but he was sitting up reading and seemed his usual self. Was quite ready to talk about his fall. He said he had decided to reopen 'the tessellation question', and had gone up on to the roof with the object of investigating the parapet from close to. Then he had slipped . . .

Derek and Myra returned in usual inane spirits, Myra clutching a miniature poodle puppy which had just been christened Nod (because Derek works for National Olibanum Distributors, Ltd.). They had visited some kennels about fifteen miles away and were full of jubilation at the oddness of the woman who ran them.

Aunt silenced them with unusual severity and reminded them it was their turn to keep watch over Uncle during the afternoon.

Asked Derek straight out, 'Do you think your Father tried to commit suicide?'

'Looks uncommon like it, doesn't it?'

'But you know he had this bee in his bonnet about that parapet. We were discussing it only last week.'

'My dear man, that was just talk. He gets these odd ideas. On Friday he happened to get another one – only that one was less funny. If we keep an eye on him for a day or two he'll soon forget all about it.'

'I don't believe he tried to make away with himself,' Myra says suddenly. Aunt looks inexplicably annoyed, Derek rudely remarks that nobody asked her opinion.

Dislike all this very much.

MONDAY

Peggy Ellis back at work; cold kept her away most of last week. She was feeling huffy most of morning because Arch Rexine had saved up a lot of filing for her instead of doing it himself.

Brightfount's existence depends mainly on files. If anything can possibly be kept and arranged in alphabetical order, Rexine sees that it is; in fact, Dave swears he keeps the leaves off his day-to-day calendar in a secret file, in case someone wants to know how many Sundays there were in February 1951. Old Gudgeon also insists on filing everything. All of which is hard luck on people like Peggy who have a job to work their way through the alphabet.

Catalogue orders tailing off. This one's done quite well, several gaps noticeable on shelves. Which is just as well, more stuff coming in all the time.

Felt worried all day.

TUESDAY

Was more or less alone in lunch hour, when in came Myra (without Nod). Very smart in grey and white check coat with grey shoes: looked more like her sister than I had noticed before. Odd to see her in Brightfount's.

She whisked about here and there, chatting most of the time. Suddenly realized how shabby the shop must look, and dark, to anyone who had not been in before.

'Come and have lunch with me, Peter,' she said. 'I want some company.' Felt rather shabby then myself, but of course agreed – by great stroke of luck I had been to cleaner's yesterday evening and got my jacket back. Had to wait till Dave came back to relieve me: he all grins and winks behind Myra's back, made the V-sign as we went out. Sometimes Dave's primitive sense of humour gets a bit much.

Myra was very agreeable: not quite her usual self. Said she got bored at 'Hatchways' with Derek away all day.

Uncle is up to-day, arm in a sling but seemingly happy enough. We both changed the subject then. After lunch, took her into the cathedral for brief look round.

'You'd wonder why on earth they ever built such a great place!' she exclaimed once, but more in awe than derision.

Returned to Brightfount's for the afternoon with some reluctance.

Old Flange, the local photographer, bustled in with large parcel of calendars with local views on.

'There you are,' he said triumphantly. 'Better get 'em out on display. Soon be Christmas, you know!'

Am generally amused to see old Flange – Mrs Callow claims that behind a veneer of almost asinine respectability he is a producer of rude photographs – but somehow he did not seem funny to-day, and the prospect of Christmas sounded dreadful.

Edith came to say there was a phone call for me. It was Myra, speaking from 'Hatchways'. She said she was warning me that Aunt Anne was on her way in to see me. She (Myra) had meant to come in yesterday to get her hair done and had forgotten all about it and Aunt had grown suspicious and had found out we had lunched together and was angry and – well, anyhow, she thought she had better warn me and I was to remember the old family motto 'Nihil Desperandum'.

All of which left me with a mixture of feelings.

We shut shop at one o'clock, and there was Aunt waiting outside.

She took me to Fuller's for lunch. We had hardly started before she began telling me how unhappy she was and how she wished I was still living with them – 'You were never any trouble, even if you did occasionally stay out rather late at nights.'

From there it was an easy step to telling me how glad she would be when Derek and Myra found a house of their own. And then the subject of Myra was launched.

Aunt Anne did not like Myra. Nor had she liked her from the start. She was sure Myra was making Derek unhappy. Myra was not to be trusted.

Interrupted to say that if that was so, I was surprised Aunt had left her in charge of Uncle Leo.

'You have no need for sarcasm, Peter. Unhappily, your Uncle seems almost to enjoy her company. I only hope you will not fall under her spell. Why exactly did she come down to see you yesterday?'

Tell her Myra said she wanted a change.

'You see! She hasn't been living with us for two months and she becomes restless. What did she have to say about me?'

'Absolutely nothing. She never even mentioned you.'

'I find that hard to believe. Well, I must go now. I hope you enjoyed your lunch. I've got to meet Mrs Howells outside the secondary school at 2.30 and she's going to drive me home in her car.'

THURSDAY

Routine at Brightfount's has always seemed to me pleasant and interesting. Days are rarely boring, weeks pass quickly. Now, suddenly, the whole business seems empty. Even Mrs Callow cannot cheer me up with her games. Suppose it is because instead of thinking of Brightfount's as life itself it has become irrelevant, something to be undergone until the next bit of living comes along.

Thought of Myra keeps worrying me. She was so nice when she came in on Tuesday: should hate to think it was with some ulterior motive. But how can you decide who's right?

Was tempted to go over there this evening. Could have done, and it was quite a decent night, but they might have thought it odd, as I don't generally turn up during the week. Also thought of phoning to say wouldn't be going over on Sunday – but have done neither. Now it's 9.40: too late for either.

FRIDAY

Spent most of morning rather absentmindedly finishing the grand sort-out of our catalogue cards, flinging out the duds. Constant interruptions occur whenever you try to get down to any job at Brightfount's.

After one such, trunk call came through for me on Arch Rexine's phone.

Derek's voice from other end announced he was speaking from N.O.D.'s London office.

'Look here, you dog, what's all this about your having a crafty affair with my wife?'

Considerably shaken, asked him where he picked up that idea from. (Feeling ghastly, blushing like fool: Rexine sitting next to me pretending to gaze at Macmillan New York catalogue with both ears standing on end.)

Derek's barking laugh in ear.

'It's all right, Peter, I didn't believe it for a moment! But Mother has got some dashed silly idea in her skull about Myra. I tell you we had a mammoth row when I got home last night. Mother said the pooch had to go – it was wetting in the lounge. What do you expect at that age? Myra put her foot down and they started a proper cat fight.'

'Was Uncle there?'

'Oh, he lapped it up! But Mother dragged you into it and got really mean. I've never heard her like it before. Maternal jealousy, I suppose. I spoke out. I said it was all a lot of stupid tosh. There wasn't half a show! Still, it certainly seems to have cleared the air. Thought I'd give you a buzz so that you'd know how things stood when you turned up at the week-end – I know Mother came over and had a poke at you.'

'Well, thanks very much for ringing, Derek.'

'Not at all, kid. All part of the bloody service.'

I hung up.

'No trouble at all, I hope?' Rexine inquired.

'Not a bit,' I said, beaming. Should have enjoyed hearing Derek hack through the family entanglements. There's nothing like a bull in a china shop to make a clean break.

SATURDAY

Felt great sense of relief on waking. Ate my three circles of breakfast sausage with relish.

Brightfount's seemed more like its old self. Even Edith, our dumb office wench, looked almost tolerable as she sneaked in the side door just before Rexine arrived.

Suppose I'm just biased in thinking Brightfount's the nicest bookshop I've ever been in; no doubt it's because I'm so at home in it. I have known other homely bookshops, quite a few. Commin's in Bournemouth is interesting, untidy place with volumes piled up on every step of every staircase; Birmingham can provide some exciting jaunts, the university towns are well furnished with bookshops. My only memory of Cambridge is being lost in Heffer's when I was about four and having to be dragged howling from their Oriental department. Oxford has fewer bookshops than might be expected, but Parker's has several intriguing bays and dead ends and corners full of books, and Thornton's is a tall maze made of little rooms, although filled with a dismaying amount of knowledge.

The best bookshops leave their doors open, at least in summer. If, directly I get inside, someone asks me what I want, I'm alarmed. Conducted tours should be unnecessary: each book bears its own sign. The books one really loves are those found by accident.

London bookshops, from the little I know of them, are either austere or dirty, with one or two austere and dirty. The most palladian of them all is Quaritch's, a single sumptuous book in each window. Wanted very much to go in there last time I was in town, but hardly liked to without a definite book to ask for. Supposing I had marched in and inquired if they possessed a 1725 edition of Bellenger's *Dispute on the Conduct of the Papacy* with erratum leaf, or some such title conjured up on the moment's spur: could I be sure that my subconscious had not played me false, and that such a book did not exist?

'Certainly, sir,' the man in the frock coat would say. 'On the third floor; we will ascend in the lift. We can offer you two copies of the 1725 edition, one in original boards from the library of the Earl of Divan and Dungeness and one in full vellum with Bellenger's signature on the flyleaf. Or we have the much rarer 1723 edition, which as you know lacks sub-title and dedication.

'We also possess Bellenger's short tract *Et Nunc Manet in Mensam Reginae*, which he wrote when tutor to Milord Happisburgh, price £125.'

And as in a horrible dream, instead of extricating myself quickly and coming away – saying perhaps that I'd wait till Penguins reprinted it – I should try and save my face, and pretend I was writing the life of Lord Happisburgh. Before I knew it, I should be staring thunderstruck at a portfolio full of unpublished documents relating to the Happisburghs from Tudor times to the War of Jenkins's Ear.

'I'd better come back to-morrow,' I should say. 'I've forgotten my reading glasses.'

'Certainly, sir. We will reserve the documents for you meanwhile, in case you should suffer the vexation of finding them purchased in the interim. Would you care to leave your address and the name of your bank?'

'Oh, a postcard care of the Post Office Savings Bank will always reach me,' and with that I should rush, weeping, for the street.

SUNDAY

Must have greeted Derek with more fervour than I usually show:

'Back there, sir! Down!' he growled, pretending to stave me off. 'Don't get too blessed cousinly or I shall think there really was something between you and Myra.'

Uncle's wrist is improving: he hopes to return to the office to-morrow. Everything seemed to have simmered down. Nod has not misbehaved again. Aunt had slight cold, seemed all right otherwise, although she said little. Myra gave me a saucy look and whispered, 'Next time you trot me round the cathedral I swear I won't tell a soul.' They were going to look at some house Uncle had heard of, so I left soon after lunch.

MONDAY

Went out with the Yells and Gyp last evening. A big field of potatoes had been mechanically harvested down by the canal behind Mr Yell's allotment. We took sacks and made quite a gleaning. It grew dark and starlit while we worked, and a thick white mist, waist high only, crept over the bare field.

On our return, Mrs Yell produced enormous cottage pie. All ate like gluttons!

Pretty slack in shop to-day. Almost like Adlestrop station, nobody left and nobody came. Notice one signed copy of *Anywhere Else on Earth* has gone. That book intrigued me; its d/w. quoted A. G. Street as saying of its horticultural author: 'He writes as he gardens.' Often wonder if this was meant to be veiled insult.

TUESDAY

With cat. orders fading and no workmen inside or outside shop, 'I think we can look forward to a peaceful week,' Dave says. 'I have several jobs I have been postponing,' and proceeds to scan through 'New Worlds Science Fiction' concealed in a publisher's catalogue.

Too good to last. Enter Gudgeon staggering under large box and Rexine following with ball of string and drawing pins. Latter's sharp eye impales Dave as he inquires mildly, 'Do you ever, in these long, pleasant days in the shop, feel you'd like to be the pride of Brightfount's, Eastwode?'

Dave admits he has never had that urge.

'Well, here's a box of a hundred calendars,' says Rexine. 'Hang a few of them about the ceiling, will you? I'll think up something else by this afternoon.'

I join in on this. Gudgeon is exhorted to make a splash with 'Equador', the brand-new card game with fun for all the family, which looks like sticking badly.

'The Christmas spirit!' groans Dave. 'Sixty more dead-stock-flogging days to Christmas.'

Christmas! It always seems to catch us unprepared. Mr B. gave quite a start of surprise when he came in and saw us actually making a beginning for the great event.

Now he is afraid Slaughterhouse won't be ready in time. What he calls 'better stuff' and prints only to go in there. Spent several hours lugging better stuff from various parts of shop, dusting or – where necessary – banging it in outside passage and carrying it into position. Mr B. sorting prints into drawers.

We soon found snag. The old books which were in the Slaughterh. in the pre-Vawsian Era, and which for months have been piled in cellar where nobody could get at them, now have no home. Originally, there was place for them in Attic, but that's now filled with last library Mr B. bought. On Thurs., Gudgeon and I have to collect more books!

WEDNESDAY
Feared as much! Out with Ruth from public library last night. She *called for me*, saying she was afraid I must be lonely all on my own in digs. Trotted me round to her house. Her dramatic group chief subject of conversation. In weak moment agreed to go with her to rehearsal on Friday night. See I shall be selling tickets at the door before I'm much older.

Rexine in good humour to-day: thought of Christmas possibly; had fit of serving in shop, which he does well when people know what they want. He got me on filling side window with Christmas cards. Thankless job. Bit draughty in there and cards apt to collapse on to one another.

'Think yourself lucky, you don't have to stick bits of cotton-wool on the window, as they do in the grocer's,' Rexine said consolingly.

Replied with mock-bitterness that that might be fun.

'Tell you what,' said Rexine. 'If you've sold all those cards by Saturday, I promise you we'll dress Gudgeon up as Santa Claus and give him a bran tub full of remainders to dish out to the kids.'

THURSDAY
Pordage, local carrier and removal man, round outside shop to collect us at 9.5. Gudgeon got in front with him, I piled in back.

House was called 'Marjoribanks House', big place at other end of town with high, shaggy laurel hedges. Large garden running wild, lawn deep in leaves, house itself rather out at magnificent elbows! Our books were in two rooms on ground floor, belonging to a Miss Prime who was selling up to go and live on south coast. Books had mostly been her brother's; he wrote *A First British History for Public Schools*.

Poor old girl wept as we took them off pile by pile. Pordage and I did the carrying while Gudgeon did the consoling.

Place was real middle-class slum. Her kitchen was little boarded-up conservatoire leading off one room, a cramped space jammed with gas cooker, sink and old wardrobe full of provisions. Earlier, more prosperous, members of family ranged the walls in solemn photographs.

Other rooms were let to other people. Figure in flowery dressing-gown opened one door to reveal what looked like set of Proust and Oxford Class. Dict. piled on top of small Prestcold with saucepans and squash bottles.

Felt v. like Vandal or Visigoth carting spoils away. Was going to admit same to Gudgeon, but he said, 'This lot should mark up well,' with such relish that I kept quiet.

Lunch: pint of milk, ham sandwich, 3d. bun. Hard up.

Lazy afternoon: Rexine out. Gone to BRS to sort out missing parcel.

Friday
Pay-day.

Pretty busy in shop, mainly owing to market day. Much milling round Christmas card display. We have good bit of last year's stock left, which has been stored in damp corner of cellar. Result: envelope flaps have all stuck themselves down. All v. fiddling, and much accidental tearing of paper in progress. We have spare envelopes, but they generally just don't fit the cards.

Did some work on Slaughterhouse. Half-finished now, and beginning to look really nice. Mr B. tickled no end; phoned up public librarian to come round and see it.

Charming little thing in about 4.45 for a Constance Spry. 'I'm funny, you know,' she confided spryly. 'There was a time when I didn't like flowers at all. But well . . . they do grow on you, don't they?'

Was delighted by this insinuation that my dusty old sports jacket might prove fertile and sprout forth daffodils.

SATURDAY

To Ruth's rehearsal last night in Women's Institute Hall. Was hard-pressed by producer to become scene-shifter, lights-operator, curtain-lifter, etc. Refused. Ruth annoyed – and not very good in her part. I vowed I would not go again, but got chatting (while Ruth was on the stage) to charming girl playing Lady Mary. Next rehearsal: Monday.

On the whole, this has been a nice quiet week at Brightfount's. Change to have no hammering, etc. Consequently we were shaken when lorry full of iron tubing drew up outside and man came in to ask Mr B. if they could erect scaffolding in outside passage.

It seems they want to repair the roof of the old Congregational Church next door. The rain has to be kept out until it is demolished early next year.

That guarantees us at least six months' pneumatic drilling!

SUNDAY

Am going home next week-end.

Everyone at 'Hatchways' seemed their usual selves to-day. Yet they all see something in each other that I don't, which worries me in a way. Must be insensitive, I suppose. Must train self to be subtle, examine people's motives, etc.

Were all invited next door to tea at Colonel Howells'. It was Julie's birthday (twenty-third) and she was home for a few days. Derek was obviously smitten with her, which struck me as rather funny.

Mr Mordicant was also there. Wondered if he was still looking for queer fish in the aquarium of post-war England, or whatever the phrase was he used. Thought we were all old-fashioned enough to disappoint him – except perhaps for Julie, who is the brilliant provincial doing wonderful technical things. Or rather *was* until she left Imperial College in London.

Now she is making hair cream by submitting oil and water to ultrasonics or something. She explained it all to us. Derek appeared to understand and invited her, by way of return, to see his car.

These motives don't need much examining.

MONDAY

Mrs Brightfount made one of her rare visits to the shop. Most of staff seemed to disappear at once, notice even Rexine extra busy in his little office. She had come to get her Christmas cards, but one of her first remarks was, 'Bernard, the shop looks a little dusty this morning.'

Actually, Bernard himself looked a little dusty. He had just been carrying some of the books Gudgeon and I collected last week up into his office for marking; the muck of 'Marjoribanks House' was slowly sifting through Brightfount's and will remain with us even when the books have all gone.

Mrs B. also noticed there were five leaves and a piece of newspaper in the porch. Mr Parsons was hailed from below to come and make a clean sweep. When she left and we breathed more easily, she popped back in to tell me a book had fallen over in the window. Did I not automatically look for things like that when I first came in? Her subconscious told her she had had to speak out about that very point before.

The book was Maugham's *Ten Novels and Their Authors*. It was face down in front of Walter Allen's *The English Novel*. Any significance, I wonder?

TUESDAY

More rehearsals of *Admirable Crichton* with Ruth last night. Most of the time it poured with rain; building has corrugated iron roof, so v. difficult to hear anything said. But they have managed to book new school hall for the actual performances, week after next. Play seems to me snobbish and out-dated, but Ruth says it happened to have right number of male and female parts for their dramatic club. Amused to see red-haired chap from Midland Bank who used to play tennis in the summer is taking small part of one of the servants.

Delicious girl playing Lady Mary, whose real name is Mary Weatherbird. She persuaded me to canvass tickets for them. Ruth trying to appear pleased at this, but looking rather frosty; now perhaps she will get someone else to hear her lines for her.

Belated but good order from last catalogue from the College of Puget Sound, Tacoma 6, a lyrically named place. Was getting on with it when in came one of those customers that *niggle* out of all proportion. He wandered round shop refusing to catch my eye, idly pulled several books off shelves, cramming them back in wrong places.

Finally he found something he wanted, an old Florin Library for two-and-six. But he was the sort who wouldn't bring it over – just stood there shuffling, coughing and clinking. Left him till I thought he would strain his throat, then served him.

He left, closing the door behind him with a soft, puget sound.

Peggy Ellis not at work to-day. She's such a quiet little mouse you hardly know she's there until she's away.

WEDNESDAY
Half-day.

'Do you *buy* books at all?'

This anxious and simple inquiry from a plump lady who looked, as Mrs Callow remarked, like a bibulous clergyman. Mr B. is going out to see her collection on Friday; it doesn't sound hopeful, but people are always vague about what they have to sell. All she could remember for sure was 'nicely bound' set of *Punch*. They *always* remember nicely bound sets of *Punch*.

Was just walking down Cross Street after we had closed when I ran into Lady Mary. On spur of moment, asked her to come and have lunch with me, which she did. Heavenly meal – but cost 9s. 8d. She has charming nose and pony tail, also good appetite. Very vivacious, and apparently half engaged to some chap in R.A.F., as she casually informed me while I was paying the bill.

Alone again, took melancholy walk over Poll's meadow towards Little Stagford. Sun strong, air bracing. Tawny and black colour of country has to be seen to be beloved. Trees at their grandest, hazels already bearing embryo lamb's tails. Was mainly preoccupied, however, with pony tails.

Half-term at nearby public school. Several bored young Pailthorpians dragged into shop by parents. Also visit from exceedingly cheery Classics master, obviously bent on showing what good fun he was. Mrs Callow served him; he bought little vellum-bound 32mo. Ovid with foul print for 8s. 6d.

Mrs Callow's comment: 'I've never Metamorphoses-ious man in my life.' Deciding the pun was too dreadful, she retreated upstairs.

Peggy Ellis back to-day. Dave did not change his expression on seeing her; wonder what motive was behind that?

Catalogued between serving. Not v. interesting lot of books on the whole, but some of the prefaces are charming. For instance, Pyke Southard's preface to his *Human Understanding in Relation to Phenomenology* concludes: 'And above all I must thank the Dean of Septuagint College, Oxford, for the loan of a deck-chair in his lovely secluded garden – how happy and fruitful were those *imminuti* after-noons! – and Mrs Hythe-Bridge, his wife, for her appearance, ever unfailing, with tea, as throat and inspiration dried. MINTON PILE, 1927.'

What a dream of quiet learning! Where's that deckchair now? I can see that gracious figure with a tray crossing the bright lawn as clearly as I see my fountain pen.

Pay-day: jolly welcome. Down to last shilling, and that's a half-crown I borrowed off Dave. While I had the money, bought copy of Mistinguett for Father, for Christmas present. The book has been so successful that I gather we will shortly have the memoirs of her father, Mr Tinguett.

Tall man in during afternoon, black coat and hat, incipient boil on back of neck. He seemed vaguely familiar, Gudgeon said he was 'a London dealer'. Somehow the words have sinister quality, or perhaps it was the way he looked quietly round the shelves. One could tell by that quick gaze this man knew all about mysterious world round about Albemarle Street, auctions at Sotheby's, etc.

Gudgeon advises: 'You don't want to be afraid of him – he's not a real bookseller. I've seen his shop. It's one of those nasty clean places in the West End with no cheap books outside and a lot of fine bindings in the window that turn out to be cigarette cases or snuff boxes.'

Mr Brightfount was not in, but the dealer chatted to Rexine and bought a little pile of books, run of Heath's *Picturesque Annual*, a Birket Foster and a couple of volumes with engravings by the Dalziel Brothers, less 10 per cent.

We get quite a few wandering booksellers in at odd times. Some are very agreeable and introduce themselves in friendly fashion when they arrive (as does Chic Anery, the American dealer, who bounds in crying, 'Don't sell *another* book till I've looked at it and offered you a better price!' and then shakes hands all round, declaring how glad he is to be back: 'We may have flying radar stations all round our shores, but we're mighty short of old used books!').

Some booksellers remain anonymous until they have picked something out and are preparing to pay: then they coolly expect a trade discount. Mr B. said to one of these types once, 'You've had our best attention for half an hour, we've dusted the dashed books for you, Eastwode there has fetched the ladder for you, we've called you "sir": you haven't been treated like trade so far and you're not going to be now. You can pay the full price or leave them, as you like.'

He was quite nettled. After some indignant grumbling, the other paid the full price and went.

Almost as soon as to-day's visitor had gone, Mr B. returned, pleased with himself, after having visited the lady with the nicely bound *Punches*. From amongst a stack of school books and Lodge's *Portraits* she had produced the first Dublin edition, 1756, of Gray's collected poems. This in very good condition and bearing on flyleaf the following couplet in a crabbed hand:

When Black *Despair this sorry* Wight *did sway,*
He only Read *his Solace in a line of* Gray.

SATURDAY

Flock of people in, despite rain. Books selling steadily enough: amazing how they go, when you think of it. We've got through seven copies of *Adventures of the World* this week alone.

A. H. Markham in. He always used to be in on Saturday morning, making a point of giving Peggy one of his peppermints, but since the Pardon business we have seen less of him. Mr B. showed him the Gray poems and he insisted that the couplet in the front was by Thomas Hood, presumably because of the puns in it. He sticks to his guns, even when Mr B. says the calligraphy is eighteenth century.

'I say that's Hood,' Markham says.

'I say that's a falsehood,' says Mr B., and is delighted to have said it.

Myra turned up midday, rather to my horror, but she insisted on paying for our lunch at the Odalisque. Also insisted we went round the cathedral again. Took my arm in very friendly way, and when I looked a bit cautious said, 'Now, now, I'm only being sisterly.'

Asked how she got on with Aunt Anne when they were thrown together all day. She wrinkled nose and said, 'I wouldn't mind at all if life went on for ever – but we haven't got long to be silly in, have we?'

She also said Derek definitely had an eye on house for them.

She also said Sheila is not enjoying her job.

November

Got home late last night. Fog delayed train.

November to-morrow, and they seem to be on different time scheme at home. Have hardly thought about Christmas, reckoned I was doing well to get Father's present so early, but here Mother is with the holiday's menus nearly all planned.

Dear Mother! I don't wonder Father gets wild with her at times. She's so impetuous. This year she is determined to have a real old-fashioned family Christmas. She wants Uncle Leo and Aunt Anne over – they stayed two years ago – and Derek and Myra, and poor old Uncle Stuart (not a real uncle) who lives on his own at Kettering.

Where we are all going to sleep does not seem to worry her. 'I'm not turning out of my bed for anyone,' Father says firmly.

'Now, dear, you know very well you positively *enjoy* sleeping on the camp bed down by the fire.'

Had lazy day and returned on earlier train than usual in case the fog got too thick.

This'll be last visit home before Christmas! That certainly makes it sound near.

Monday

Changed the Bottomley Place window. Pestered by a four-year-old who watched me with fascination, tapping occasionally on glass with giant lollipop. From his viewpoint I must have been quite watchable: window is cunningly constructed to be deep enough to make it necessary to get in it, low enough to make it impossible to stand up in it and narrow enough to make it impracticable to squat in it. Dave, in fact, once described it as 'a strait-jacket with a glass front'.

Managed quite decent display of Christmas cards. Really odd how about this time of year people suddenly want little pictures of Swiss valleys, Scotch mountains, camels and Cologne cathedral. Must be a thwarted travel-urge showing itself.

No – can't be that – there's just as much interest in puppies wearing hats, eighteenth-century women in eighteenth-century gardens and horrible red carpets by roaring red fires.

We've got a new line this year, but by and large our stock is a terribly conservative one. Shaking his head despairingly over the fleets of snow-bound stage-coaches, Dave says, 'Not a space-ship among 'em!'

Actually we have one or two with television on, but they're all comic: 'A Merry Xmas and a Hobley New Year' – that kind of thing.

Tuesday

Odd as it seems to us, Gudgeon has relations. He has, especially, an infant nephew in Winchelsea of whom he is proud. Yesterday morning Gudgeon went out and bought him a woolly dog for a birthday next week. We irritated him by professing not to recognize what species of animal it was; Peggy Ellis guessed lamb, Mrs Callow horse, I cat. Gudgeon became very superior, would not let Mrs C. cuddle it, put it in Rexine's office above the obsolete set of Nelson's Encyclopaedia, well out of our way.

Unfortunately, he forgot the unhappy creature when we were going home. This morning Mr Parsons greeted him with a kind of melancholy triumph in his voice: 'That there Brightfount terrier of yours has been in trouble during the night; the rats have had his leg off.'

The toy had indeed been nibbled by mice, and sawdust was scattered about Rexine's office. Rexine none too pleased, Gudgeon furious. As senior assistant, he is the only one of the staff who dares make a scene. Tackling Rexine did little good, he merely said we had always had mice and that in any case we weren't supposed to be a toy shop.

When Mr B. came in about ten, he got long diatribe about 'filthy working conditions' and he promised to ring up a ratcatcher. Gudgeon placated!

Peggy v. nervous after this, refused to go down to the cellar for her tea; Mr Parsons vowed he had seen a huge big rat down there.

WEDNESDAY
The life of the town (such as it is) generally flows by Brightfount's front door leaving us undisturbed, but to-day we had a visit from Owen Owen. Not only is he the leading local draper, but he is a town councillor. Not only is he a town councillor, but he is a poet. Before he left Wales he published a little volume of verse in Welsh and, since he came here, Shire and Gantlet published his *Prayer for the Little Housing Estates*. We have a stock of this book.

Owen Owen is pompous but charming.

'I dare say I'm the only person who buys my poems, aren't I?' he asks wistfully.

'We sold a copy to an American in the summer,' says Mrs Callow, which is perfectly true.

'Why now, that's a long way for a little book to travel,' he exclaims, pleased as Punch. 'You didn't happen to have the gentleman's name and address did you now, or I could write him a letter?'

When Mrs Callow shakes her head, he says, 'Never mind, my dear – but it would have been another link in the cultural bond between our two nations.'

He bought a couple of little books before leaving. Mrs C. said he had tiny shopping list on which he had written neatly:

Carol, The Christmas
—'— Lewis

Thursday

Very busy. Good lot of customers in; Christmas does make them look a bit more intelligent.

Sold last copy of *In Utmost Krutchestan*, at last. It's pity someone doesn't tell these publishers how difficult it is to sell the last of six copies of a book. When you've got a stack of them and they look fresh, they go quite easily. Then the last one sticks. After you've dusted it once a week for two or three years you begin to wish the author had never left home.

Friday

Pay-day. Went and ate really large lunch. Shocking wet morning, flood of customers with dripping umbrellas – quite a lake under the card counter.

Rodent operative in yesterday, although I didn't see him. Dave said Gudgeon advanced and shook him fervently by the hand saying, 'I welcome you in the name of all stuffed things, including Arch Rexine, our junior partner' – but you can't always believe Dave.

Anyhow, little piles of white powder now dot the shop and Peggy has taken precaution of sprinkling a little in her coat pocket.

Had funniest Guy Fawkes day I've enjoyed for years. The Yells' neighbour in No. 59 is pale yellow fellow called Arraway, or it may be Harroway. He has gigantic wife and two noisy little girls of nose-running age. Strife existed between Yells and Arraways even before advent of children, whose ability to be heard easily through walls did nothing to heal the breach.

Arraway, however – who seems inoffensive enough to me, and grins in sickly fashion when we meet – always throws large firework party on Guy Fawkes day. Yells always watch this from behind curtains of what is now my room. They came up this evening as usual, directly they heard Arraway mustering his forces in the garden.

Besides his own brood, he had invited in the two small boys from the house the other side of his and a family called Turner, which consisted of two young women, a babe who should have been in bed, a little girl in rubber boots and a self-assured teenager with an unlighted cigarette in his mouth who assisted Arraway to light the blue fuses.

Amid much laughing, shouting and crying, two large boxes of fireworks were brought out.

'He's got more than ever this year!' Mrs Yell announces in horrified excitement. 'Where he gets the money from . . .'

'They'll see you, Vera, if you don't keep well back,' says Mr Yell, with equal excitement.

And it is exciting. The glass gets smeary with our excitement and has to be frequently rubbed.

'Come on then, let's get organized!' roars Arraway. He plonks one box down, selects a large catherine wheel, pins it to a post (the Arraway garden is full of posts!) and lights it. It fizzes round merrily, scattering sparks, the children shriek with pleasure – and next moment the firework box below is also alight.

Arraway emits sound like a small bull, seizes up box, and next moment is dashing about with it, bathed in various colours of fire. Rocket hurtles past his ear like serpent, plunges into grass and writhes hissing over ground. Children all howling, Yell banging me over and over on shoulder saying, mesmerized, 'The silly clumsy fool! The silly clumsy fool!'

A shilling cannon exploding in box blows it from Arraway's hands. He pulls off overcoat, flings it on to blaze and jumps on it.

One final explosion and the fireworks are under control. The children are another matter. The sight of father apparently on fire has terrified them, and they have to be bundled inside, screaming.

Arraway and self-assured teenager begin by torchlight to pick any unexploded fireworks out of the long grass. These they light, watched by women from shelter of scullery door. Both are especially nonchalant after the mishap, stroll round with roman candles and vesuviuses in their hands, belching fire.

And in a flash they had managed to set the second box of fireworks alight! It was against the wall of the house, some feet away from them, so how they did it, goodness knows. But a second later the back of the house was bathed in violent light and the air full of explosions and flares. It was worth walking miles to see!

Mr and Mrs Arraway exchanged a few sharp words and they all dashed inside, slamming the door and leaving the fireworks to burn themselves out. We three went hilariously downstairs to high tea; sound of furious quarrelling through the wall setting the seal to the Yells' enjoyment.

SATURDAY

Peering out of bathroom window could see pile of burnt-out fireworks and trampled overcoat in next door garden.

Cold but marvellous day. Hope it's decent to-morrow. Bagger's Dune always looks glorious in deep autumn hues, should like a walk out there.

Had another look at Owen Owen's poems. Quite pleasant little book. On title-page, under his name, it says in brackets, 'The Swan of Swansea'. For the sake of alliteration, he's to be congratulated that he wasn't born in Henley.

No sign of mice anywhere in shop. Rexine said the only real test would be for Gudgeon to buy another toy dog, a remark not well received.

After nasty experience this afternoon shall be careful in future about airing opinions. Rather terrible little man, smelling of scent and cigars, came in and asked me if we had got Denzil Odgers' book called *Britain's Witches and Wizards*. Had never heard of it, but amiably went and looked on shelves.

'We've got this,' I said, handing him Christine Hole's *Witchcraft in England*. 'It's much better.'

'Oh, is it? Better than Denzil Odgers'?'

Didn't like his tone of voice, so said firmly, 'Undoubtedly.'

'Well, I don't agree with you,' he said nastily, 'and I'm Denzil Odgers.'

Silly of me not to have guessed, I suppose. There was one obvious clue: he not only knew author and title, but publisher and price – in other words, it had to be the author!

It left me in a nasty Hole.

Apart from an uneasy idea that one day Dave will really infuriate Rexine and get himself sacked, I seem to get a stable feeling from Brightfount's. Brightfount's will never go bust; it will never make anyone's fortune. As Miss Harpe, who left last spring, once indignantly remarked to a customer accusing us of inefficiency, the pale face of the bookseller's assistant is the backbone of literary Britain. Nothing seems likely to change, for better or worse.

Odd, therefore, to find that in the mere fortnight since I last visited 'Hatchways', a lot seems to have happened there. Nod has doubled his size and was tearing up and down the hall with one of Uncle's old hats when I arrived. Aunt and Uncle had little to say to each other. Derek has actually bought a house much nearer London.

'Devil's cheap, it was!' he told me. 'Worth twice the price – valuable and historic old property, no kidding. You know what that means: no damn bathroom or lavatory.'

They are having a new wing built on and a staircase pulled down and hope to move in next February.

But the most interesting remark came from Aunt Anne just before I was leaving. She took me out to the old wash-house which is now an apple store and presented me with some Autumn Pearmains and half a dozen Barnack Beauties, favourites of mine, although they taste even better after being stored a little longer.

'Peter, although I have no desire to encourage you in ingratitude,' she began, 'you really must not be too effusive in your thanks. It is a fault – one you are prone to. It is a sign of an uncontrolled upbringing.'

Apologize.

'Yes. It reminds me of an occasion when Lawrence was staying with your Uncle and me in the Lower Wickham days. We had been in to see Mr Brightfount, although as you know the shop was Mr Gaspin's then—'

'You mean Lawrence actually went into Brightfount's?'

'Am I not just telling you so? And as we were stepping out – I shall never forget it – quite a poor man came in. He was only a working-class person, but he held the door open nicely for us, and as we passed through, Lawrence said, "Thank you."

'The poor man replied, "Thank *you*, sir!" and Lawrence was so cross he turned back and said, "You have nothing to be grateful to me for."'

'And this happened in Brightfount's doorway?'

'Peter, I am trying to impress the moral, not the location, upon you.'

MONDAY

Entered the old place with more respect this morning. Wonder who else of the famous have been in without our knowing? Of course, there's Sir Roger Wynd and Owen Owen, and Dave swears he once served Arthur C. Clarke, but – Lawrence . . .

Must ask Mr B. about him some time, but to-day did not seem very convenient, as he was very busy and had into the bargain a cough like the bark of a Great Dane.

Was sitting downstairs with Yells in the evening when Gyp came in from the yard with my old shaving brush in his mouth. Don't know where he dug it up from, but certainly did not want it myself, and told the old dog he could keep it. Mr Yell said it might 'come in handy for odd painting jobs about the house', and snatched it from him. Gyp retreated under table with melancholy long withdrawing roar.

TUESDAY

Dropped some books in at public library, saw Ruth. She now is not speaking to me. There's gratitude, after I've been selling tickets for her wretched play. This great event comes off Thurs. and Fri. Mr and Mrs Yell are coming with me; Aunt bought couple of tickets, but don't suppose she and Uncle will turn up. The Callows are also putting in an appearance.

Phone rang this morning; Edith, happening to be down in shop, answered it, said, 'Just a moment' and went off to get Rexine. I was serving, but behind customer's back our dumb office wench made cutting movement across throat with extended finger, which is her elegant way of indicating Mrs Brightfount is in offing.

Guessed what was on. When Rexine answered phone, could almost hear crisp voice at other end say, 'I'm keeping Bernard at home to-day.'

Odd type, Rexine. When he announces to us that Mr B. will not be in, he says in solemn voice, 'Mrs Brightfount says her subconscious tells her he is in danger of bronchitis unless he rests.' He must know that when Dave imitates Mrs B. the realism of the effect depends on the frequency with which he says 'my subconscious tells me . . .'

Terribly easy to parrot a phrase, especially in a bookshop. Gudgeon, as becomes his age, trots several stereotyped sentences out regularly to customers. 'We don't really get much call for that kind of book,' is his favourite. Dave starts all his explanations with, 'Well you see, madam, the thing is . . .' Often find myself saying, 'I know the book but haven't seen a copy lately.' These things come all too automatically.

Reminds me of Gudgeon's story about a bookseller's famous last words. He looked up, saw the figure of Death approaching and asked, 'Can I help you, sir?'

WEDNESDAY

Boss still away. Had to help Gudgeon with *Clique* orders. Do enjoy seeing these cards from all over the country, try and picture what their shops are like. And when the books we order from them arrive, they are often wrapped in the local paper: *Bournemouth Echo, Bolton Evening News, Oxford Mail, Dereham and Fakenham Advertiser.*

We were advertising this week for Shaw's *Everybody's Political What's What* (quite by mistake, because after the advert. had gone in we found two copies on one of those dim shelves behind the Slaughterhouse where nobody ever looks). We got fifteen quotes, from 'good copy, 3s. post free' to 'first edition near mint in dust wrapper, 22s.'.

Mr B. back in action, still with his Great Dane bark, but looking glad to be back.

Charming little sample of stubbornness by History section today. A crate-load of books for disposal from man in Kirk Muxloe arrived on Monday; they had been priced and Gudgeon was sticking our nasty little black labels in them and sorting them slowly away.

He had no sooner started than customer in mac detached himself from the Penguins and went over to see what Gudgeon had got. As Gudgeon left the pile he was working on, the customer would slip in, and then Gudgeon would come back from other side, solemnly pushing his way in without a word. Gudgeon can be v. stubborn. Finally he took an armful and went up the ladder with them, putting them on a top shelf.

Directly he came down again, the customer went up the ladder. Gudgeon sorted and arranged noisily beneath, until a copy of Artz's *Revolution and Reaction* caught him on the top of the head.

He looked up with a scowl. Customer smiled placatingly, said, 'It's all right, I want to buy it.'

This quite amusing to watch. Their timing was so good. They might have been representing Curiosity and Inflexibility in a medieval mime. Wonder nobody has written a book ballet – could be charming. Escape book whirls on to stage: orchestra plays a few bars. Enter Undersea Diving book to flood of music. These execute a *pas de deux* while others like them, appearing from both sides at once, almost fill the stage. Almost: for a thin line of little blue ballerinas, representing World Classics, gradually replaces the first group and is joined by a sprightly troupe of First Novels, who pirouette briefly and are gone. Stately rows of Memoirs glide on, followed closely by the slender, childish figures of some Modern Poets. All are swept away by bounding, leaping Best Seller.

The *prima ballerina*, the heroine, is a Ballet book dressed in white and edited by Arnold Haskell. The villain of the piece, a demon called Illiteracy, is black-clad with a twelve-inch screen over his face. Eventually he is defeated by the hero (Mr United Publishers), who takes the little Ballet book on his shoulder and floats off with her across the perilous Lake of Royalties to Circulation Castle.

The scene fades and the music ends with the quiet notes of a fiddle.

Can't think what has made me all musical of a sudden. Must be because Edith was given the afternoon off to go up to London and see the new mammoth musical, *Iphigenia on Ice* by Goethe and Oscar Hammerkratz VI, which has just opened.

FRIDAY
Pay-day.

Had the chance just after lunch of asking Mr Brightfount what he remembered of D. H. Lawrence, if he bought anything or not. He looked blank, said he never recalled Lawrence coming in at all: Uncle used to come in a lot, but never – as far as Mr B. could recollect – with anyone like Lawrence; where did I get that idea?

Definitely odd this. Mr B. has good memory.

SATURDAY
Mr and Mrs Yell came with me to see *Admirable Crichton*. Nobody fell off the stage.

It was disappointing in other ways, too. The night was freezing and something had gone wrong with the heating system, so we sat huddled together shivering. At one point or another, everyone forgot their lines. Must admit Ruth was not bad as Tweenie; my dear Lady Mary was wonderful. Have at last found out the name of the chap from the Midland Bank: Glover. Not that it matters, but it's nice to know.

Introduced Lady Mary immediately after performance to Mrs Yell, who told me later, 'I'm sure in me heart of hearts she's a very nice girl, but what a lot of make-up she had got on.'

Presumably Mrs Yell's heart of hearts is in the same place as Mrs Brightfount's subconscious, but can't help feeling the former is the warmer spot, for all her faults.

Man we call our thief in to-day just before closing. Have not

128

seen him for some weeks. Shop very crowded. Mrs Callow sure she spotted him tucking something under his jacket, grew very excited, grabbed Rexine by the arm.

'No good panicking,' says Rexine, ultra-calm. 'What did he take?'

'Oh, look, he's going! Can't you—'

'What did he take?'

'Something off the front table. *The Curse-word is Porridge* – I mean, *The Password is Courage*.'

They were too late. The bird had flown: not a sign of him in Cross Street; he must have known we saw him. I'll bet my *Admirable Crichton* programme to a curse of porridge that we don't see *him* again.

SUNDAY

Sharp, fine day, sun shining and the land looking rich and dark. Grand to be alive-o! Cycled singing all the way to 'Hatchways' – and when I got there Sheila was in the kitchen peeling potatoes!

She looked my idea of really sweet; astonishing how much like Myra she is. Told her what a pleasant surprise it was to see her. She has given up her job, arrived by train last night.

Derek: 'You needn't worry, my girl. With looks like you've got and pull like I've got, I'll soon get you a cushy number at National Olibanum!'

Had odd feeling that Aunt was not too pleased to have Sheila. Apparently she did arrive more or less unannounced, but begin to suspect Aunt is rather sinister character. Still, poor dear is getting on: quite understandable that she does not want too much extra work.

Had no chance to raise Lawrence question, for which I was glad. Derek drove the two sisters, Nod and me over to see their new house at Epley. He is obviously very proud of it, although he modestly declares, 'It may be of no period in particular, but at least there's a beam here and there to bash your head on.'

He and Myra climbed into the false roof to investigate some suspected loose tiles. Sheila and I were alone on the bare, forlorn landing. From the way she looked at me I knew she understood the way I was looking at her. With that detached feeling of inevitability, I was putting my arms round her. She said something – just cannot recall what, because at that moment a bellow from above said, 'Hey, you two, stop necking directly our backs are turned!'

Sensitive bod, Derek: such a poetic choice of words, too.

MONDAY
Beastly wet day, Mrs Yell, my landlady, had to bang on my door twice before I got up. Result was, I cut things a bit fine and arrived late at work. Sneaked down side passage, rolling up mack under my arm as I went, but found only Peggy Ellis in shop and stove not lit. Peggy looking v. excited.

'Do you know what?'

'What?' I asked.

'The thingme in the what's-it's come down. Rexine's in a fearful stew.'

Peggy is not the most lucid of conversationalists, but I soon discovered what she meant. The cistern out at the back, in our smallest room, had collapsed during the night. When Mr Parsons arrived first thing, he found a flood of water running across the floor by the old kitchen and down the stairs into his cellar.

As far as Dave and I were concerned, this proved blessing in disguise, as there was little to do in shop, no customers, and we were sent downstairs to help mop up. This took good while.

Gudgeon and Mr B. upstairs cataloguing as hard as they can go – which in Gudgeon's case is not very hard.

To-day Sheila drove up to London with Derek, going to look for a job.

TUESDAY
Our flood yesterday has brought down big section of plaster in the cellar.

'You know what that means,' says Mr Parsons, '– more workmen down here, falling over the books. Next thing we know, old Vaws'll be round here again.'

Think he is particularly grieved because defunct bit of wall always served as his notice-board. It really looks odd not to go down there and be confronted with the poster for the Festival of Britain and the photo of Monica Dickens. There were also a number of personal notes that lent a homely air: 'Nobody at home at 10 Cedermere Gardens from Fri.-Mon. inclusive', 'All parcels for Mrs Willoughby-Smith to go Registered', 'Please DO NOT empty tea-leaves into waste paper sack', 'No more credit for Major Jacks'.

They were as much a part of the permanent furniture of Brightfount's as the chap who comes in every Saturday afternoon to read our set of Casanova.

We took only £3 18s. 3d. yesterday, and that included 6s. 6d. Mrs Callow put in for her Christmas cards. I should think today we did even less. Dave says cheerfully he gives us six months before we are in the thick of a closing-down sale. Mr B. does not look much perturbed; a traveller was in and Mr B. was ordering from him quite cheerfully. Went past Pardon's in the lunch hour, and saw Reggie was serving one solitary customer – looking as if he had the cold to end all colds and trying to sell copy of *Always Healthy, Always Handsome*, poor man.

WEDNESDAY
Better day, more customers in.

Had two rather charming elderly women in Slaughterhouse, buying prints. Produced nice little water-colour of roses from flower portfolio; ladies seemed mildly interested in it, so started giving them bit of sales talk, pointing out how really exquisitely the sheen on the leaves was managed, what delicate colour, etc., etc. . . . . Suddenly realized in middle of it all – just when they were getting a bit excited – that what I was saying was perfectly true, and painting was, as I claimed, a real little gem.

Became overwhelmed with desire to have the roses myself. Stopped pep-talk at once. Said offhandedly, 'Still, the general effect is a bit amateurish,' and tried to interest them in some Bartolozzis. But they still clutched the roses, cooing slightly. Said no more, but was much relieved when finally they had something else instead, a rather hideous lily with a toucan in the background. Took water-colour to Rexine, who let me have it for seven and six cost. Horribly broke now till Friday.

Considered going over to 'Hatchways' for afternoon, then decided better not. Considered writing Sheila note, but decided against that, too. Thought I would write her poem: after all, she need never see it.

Don't seem to have the knack as I used to. Ah to be twenty-one again! What temerity I had then! Stuck with nothing but 'azalea' to rhyme with 'failure'; and then gave it up.

THURSDAY

Two more travellers in to-day. While one was waiting to go in and see Mr B. he told us very good joke about little boy and the Polish border. Can't help getting an idea of each publishing firm from their representatives, but am always sorry agreeable Gollancz man doesn't go round in yellow jacket.

Travellers always seem to me to be the muscles which keep gangling body of the book trade working. They bind whole thing together, give us sense of contact with the region above and below our belt. Some of them are quite exotic characters: there's Mr Roath of Stodding's, who fought (and beat) a Birmingham bookseller in his own shop, and Mr Jones of Five Shires Press, who writes cowboys under the name of Chesapeake Lewis.

Mr Cordell was in today, very interesting man. Been on the road since before first World War. He knows lot about the old booksellers. Was telling us last time he was here of Percy Dorge.

'He had a shop in Charing Cross Road then – this was before he more or less retired and went to Worthing – and I remember going in one day and finding him sitting in the back of the shop with his trousers rolled up and his feet in a mustard bath.

'"Ah, Cordell," he said, "don't mind this, will you? Come and sit down and show me what you've got – not that I'm in a buying mood to-day."

'And a customer came in while I was there and asked for one of Dean Inge's books, and old Dorge said, "There's a copy above that run of the Library of Anglo-Catholic Theology," and when the customer didn't seem to be cottoning on, he said to me, "Here, Cordell, you show him: make yourself useful!"'

FRIDAY
Pay-day; feel pretty flush again, particularly as new cistern is now installed.

Soaking wet, but plenty of customers about, to-day being market day.

Shall soon have been in book trade four years. Amazing how the time has gone, and I don't seem to have learnt much. To be a real bookseller is very hard job – wonder if I'll ever be one?

It's really quite romantic job. Still become excited when I get the chance to help Mrs Callow or Rexine undoing parcels of new books. Out they slide, bright, fresh jackets, loaded with their reviewers' golden opinions and their publishers' blessings, full of multitudinous opinions and ideas. I admit they soon become less inspiring: once they've hung about the shop for six months and the jacket's tousled at the top, then they've overstayed their welcome – but when they are still hot off the press, what more intoxicating than the sight, feel and smell of them?

SATURDAY
Mr Yell, who is 'handy with his hands', has cut down old picture frame to fit my roses, and they now hang in my room. Persuaded Mrs Yell to let them go over bed in place of oleograph entitled 'What's the matter with My Daddy?' This Victorian little human drama is apparently too precious to be 'put away', so is squeezed behind the door next to photo of Mrs Yell's sister Grace, who married a Canadian.

Casanova man in; now half-way through Vol. III. We don't mind, really, but to-day he had the sauce to borrow paper bookmark off Peggy.

SUNDAY

Funny thing – as I was cycling along Graves St Giles road, Piggy
Dexter and his sister Susie were coming in opposite direction; with
them was Glover, the ginger chap from the Midland Bank. He had
the cheek to ask me how Avril was!

They want me to go out with them on Wednesday.

As we were chatting, fire-engine hurtled past; Piggy said he thought
for a moment they were after Glover's hair, but apart from that we
paid no attention.

When I got to 'Hatchways', however, there was the engine in the
drive with half the village hanging round outside and hoses leading
into the house. No sign of smoke, but dozens of cheerful firemen in
shining hats walking about.

Sound of Aunt crying led me to sitting-room. There she was,
Derek comforting her, Myra standing looking uncomfortable and
cuddling Nod, Sheila just looking uncomfortable. Latter definitely
cheered when she saw me. Has most *innocent* face.

A strip of wallpaper by the fireplace was blackened, several yards
of the tall window curtain had been burnt, one pane of glass was
cracked. They all, except Sheila, started to explain what had happened.

It had been Uncle's doing.

Every year he collects and dries bullrushes to serve as spills to
light his pipe with. These are kept in an old wicker wastepaper basket
which stands for that purpose by the fireplace. After using one of
these spills, he carelessly put it back in the basket without extinguishing
it properly. Next minute, the whole caboodle was on fire.

Uncle Leo drops his Sunday paper into the hearth – where it
promptly catches fire! – and flings open the window to throw the
basket out. The draught fans the blaze and the curtain bursts into
flames. Shouting for help, he throws the basket out and leaps over
the sill himself to grab a bucket of liquid manure standing nearby.

Getting back in to extinguish the blaze, he upsets the manure into
one of the leather armchairs. Fortunately, Derek has arrived on the
scene. He pulls down the curtain and beats out the flames with a
rug.

It took me some time to gather this story. Aunt Anne was mildly hysterical and obviously thought poor Uncle had been attempting suicide again, this time with the intention of taking them all with him to a better world.

The firemen were just going when Dr Thorley arrived, although Sheila had phoned for him when she dialled the fire brigade. He had just got Aunt well soothed when she sat up and said, 'I'm sure I shan't dare to sleep in this house to-night. I'm positive I can smell something burning *now!*'

'It's the scent of it still lingering in your nostrils,' the doctor assured her.

'It's not, you know,' Sheila said. 'It's the lunch!'

Uncle did not appear for lunch. He went out when the chaos was at its height and did not return till mid-afternoon. We had a constrained tea together.

Came back here pretty early, Sheila walking some of the way with me. She has got a job, although not with Derek, and a room in Victoria. She is to work with Church Adoption Society and will do visiting and care of children.

'But I shall feel awfully lonely,' she said. 'I've never been on my own before. You will write, won't you?'

Most pathetic.

Kissed her just before a shower of rain came on.

MONDAY

'I really can't imagine how you remember what you have in stock!' the lady customer with the small boy exclaims admiringly.

'Oh, I don't know, madam,' Gudgeon answers modestly. 'It's partly a matter of training.' She had asked him for a fishing book, *This Coarse Predilection*, and he replied at once that we had not got it.

'But you have so many volumes here,' she continues. 'They must run into thousands and thousands! (Come here, Billy!)'

'Oh, more than that, madam,' says Gudgeon, more gratified, more vague, than before.

'Well, I think it's very clever – Come *here*, Billy!'

'But, Mummy, look on this table! *This Coarse Pre-, Pre-* . . . Isn't this the book we wanted?' fishing it triumphantly up in his interfering little hands.

'It's not only *me*, it lets the whole shop down,' Gudgeon complains to Mr Brightfount after this one minute tragedy. 'We should all be informed when you smuggle fresh second-hand stock in.'

'Smuggled, be dashed!' says Mr B. 'I was here till 8.30 on Saturday night marking that lot.'

Dave warned Gudgeon seriously that he would be getting the push if he spoke to his employers like that. But as senior assistant Gudgeon is allowed a little more rope than the rest of us; occasionally he almost hangs himself with it.

TUESDAY
Christmas creeping up. Popped out during tea break and got Mother very nice patent coffee brewer.

Wrote to Sheila. Pulling my writing pad out, found Avril Dodd's letter tucked in the back. Really meant to answer it, but never did. Destroyed it rather furtively: with Sheila am making new start.

WEDNESDAY
Woken about 6.30 with the feeling of terror and Mrs Yell banging on the bedroom door.

'What's the matter? Is the house on fire?'

'You were having a nightmare, that's what's the matter,' she called. 'You were calling out something awful!'

It certainly had been horrible, although it just seems muddled now. Must be like Swedenborg and keep dream diary by bedside.

It was about the letter I wrote last night to Sheila. I had begun it 'Dear Avril,' and was trying to explain the mistake to Sheila. Said to her, 'I really love you, I never loved Avril at all,' and then real-ized that it was not Sheila I was talking to but Avril herself.

We were standing in Pardon's: Reggie Pardon and someone like Arch Rexine were there, and they kept piling books up between us, and I said to Avril, 'Can't you stop them?' She answered me, and it was something frightfully important, something my life depended on, only everything was so muddling I forgot it at once.

I pushed somebody out of the way to get to her. I was shouting. Then the whole thing dissolved and somehow it wasn't me at all but my brother. Yet it was not even quite him, but something masquerading as him.

It was like a science fiction story Dave once told me about, where creatures from another world changed themselves into the guise of men, with evil intent.

Arrived early at Brightfount's.

Dave and Edith both arrived late. Rexine was quite objectionable to Dave, but it's like water off a duck's back to him!

All v. interested, by the way, to see that Pardon's has started to advertise in local paper with nasty little jingles. Saturday's was something about

> *If there's any special book you want to read,*
> *Pardon's will be glad to fill your need.*

Wonder if it was Reggie or Babs Pardon composed this gem, or if it took both of them to do it! By the evidence of their window, the need is for puppets, fountain pens and peepshow books.

Dear Mrs C., in whom the quality of mercy is somewhat strained at times, had been inspired to do some composing on their behalf. Perhaps her best effort was

> *If you wants a book got ere your arteries hardens,*
> *Don't ask in vein, just ask in Pardon's.*

Shop closed in afternoon. Cycled out to Bishops Linctus with Piggy Dexter and Ginger Glover, who is apparently known to his more literary friends as 'Red Gauntlet'. Rained most of the time, and was definitely freezing when I got back here – first severe frost of winter.

Mrs C. not here when shop opened. Rexine's eye fiercely on watch – but foiled because she never came at all.

One odd type walked in to-day and marched over to our old bindings. He wore new yellow suede shoes, an old overcoat and an air of superiority. After a while he selected a calf-bound volume called *The Romish Horse-leech* (1674) – perhaps the title attracted him! – and took it over to Peggy Ellis.

'That will be fifteen shillings, please,' she told him.

This irritated him. 'What, for a battered old thing like that?' he asked. He attempted to argue and then remarked bitterly, 'It's too expensive for me, I tell you straight. And I'll tell you why it's too expensive. It's you middlemen putting the price up. People ought to get together and cut you middlemen out – they ought to get their books straight from the factory!'

'I've never been so insulted,' Peggy said afterwards. 'Calling me a middleman . . .'

His comment certainly did not reveal much knowledge of the book trade. Hard to tell whether thorough knowledge or thorough ignorance lay behind another customer's inquiry: 'You do keep Autobiography in with Fiction, do you?'

FRIDAY

Poor Mrs Callow limped in this morning. There was ice on the roads yesterday and she fell off her bike at the corner of Canon's Walk. She has to go to hospital for X-ray to-morrow.

Pay-day.

Dave made an ass of himself. Mr B. had got him on cataloguing with Gudgeon upstairs. Dave was nicely settled with paper and a pile of stodgy stock when military gent came up and asked him for something. Instead of bothering to get up, Dave sat where he was and answered.

'Confound it, man,' said the military gent, 'haven't you the civility to rise when you address a customer?'

Dave had a flash of stupid inspiration. He lurched painfully to his feet with a grimace that indicated he was bravely making the best of things and said, 'Sorry, sir – old war wound in the leg, you know – Burma '44 . . . Makes me a bit slow at times.'

'Oh, I say!' military gent exclaims, appalled and quite taken in. 'I do apologize to you, sir. Of course I had no idea . . .'

'Quite all right, quite all right, sir, of course you hadn't.'

'Neither had any of us,' said Mr Brightfount grimly, when the customer had retreated in confusion – he had arrived without Dave's noticing in time to catch the gist of this conversation. 'I want to hear no more of that sort of joke in this shop, Eastwode.'

SATURDAY

'How's your poor old leg, Dave?'

For some unknown reason, Dave ignored my friendly morning greeting and continued upstairs whistling his favourite tune, 'That's My Gal Ignani'. We didn't see much of him all day: he was getting quietly on with the cataloguing.

Mrs C. has twisted kneecap or something. She came in to tell us she has to lie up 'for at least a fortnight'. Hard luck at this time, but Mr Callow is going to stay off work for a while to look after her, so it will be a holiday for them.

'Where's the one-man purge?' she asked.

'Rexine? He's out; probably gone to the dentist,' Dave said. Funnily enough, he was right. When Rexine came back, he mentioned to Peggy Ellis that he had had a filling loose for a few days! So we hope for a less turbulent atmosphere now – always provided Dave behaves himself!

Rexine and Mr B. had conference during tea break, after which Mr B. told us, 'I'm going to get someone in to lend us a hand next week, as Mrs Callow will be away. One of my wife's cousins will be glad to come, I know.'

Whereupon I received a crippling kick from Dave behind the counter. When Mr B. had gone, Dave said, 'You mind you wash behind the ears on Monday, kid! That'll be Miss Toplady! She came and helped out five Christmases ago.'

'Oh,' I said uneasily, 'is she fierce?'

'No, nothing like that. She's – well, simple but effective. If Rexine ever had a mother she'd be like Miss Toplady.'

'You mean – strict?'

'No, unmarried.'

November–December

Yesterday was foul weather, to-day fine. Sun shone in clear blue sky all day, land looking handsome and alert. Saw a heron sunning himself by Bagger's Bridge.

Derek has not seen Sheila since she started work; he eats at a canteen, so does not even lunch with her. Myra had a note from her saying her digs were comfortable and she was happy; no mention of me.

Traces of fire at 'Hatchways' more or less eliminated – new pane of glass installed, etc. But fancy slight aroma of manure still hangs over the lounge.

Was determined to have a word alone with Uncle Leo. Over lunch he was cheerfully discussing the little brick railway stations on the old L.N.E.R. line from Norwich to Peterborough. 'That was where we should have stopped,' he says.

That could mean so many things. Did not gather whether he meant that he and Aunt should have got out there, or if he wished they lived in that part of England, or if he meant that civilisation had reached a sort of harmony when the stations were built. Did not ask him. Nor did anyone else.

Got a chance to speak to him later. The others were engaged in overhauling some of Derek's belongings which have just arrived from

142

Southampton. Uncle was putting on his coat for a stroll and I joined him.

'I'm going over to see Alleluia Pickles,' he said. 'He's the oldest inhabitant since poor old Mrs Cocker gave up the ghost. Some day I'd like to find a house with as grand a magnolia in the garden as he's got.'

Asked him if he was not settled at 'Hatchways'.

'We've lived here quite a while . . . I like it, y'know, but it's not perfect. Houses are like people – you never find 'em perfect. Anne seems to like it.'

'You used to review books for the *Journal and Advertiser*, didn't you?'

'Years ago – thirty years ago. I had an idea I would pursue a literary career.'

This was the moment. Asked him if he had ever met D. H. Lawrence.

'No, the only famous people I've ever met are Gilbert Murray and Richard le Gallienne. He bought a house off us once; Father handled it . . .'

'You've never had Lawrence to stay with you?'

'Goodness gracious, no, Peter! Has Bernard Brightfount been pulling your leg?'

Did not say Aunt Anne had repeatedly told me so. Could hardly say anything. Left him at Pickles' door, returned for my bike and cycled back without seeing the others.

The fact must be faced: Aunt is a thumping liar!

MONDAY

Ralph Mortlake, local dramatic critic, flounced in. He did not really want to buy a book, although he picked up a second-hand Penguin just for the look of things. Am sure he only came to tell Mr B. – in voice loud enough to reach Peggy Ellis and me – that he had just had a half-hour play accepted for commercial television.

This certainly does make it all sound horribly near. Suppose it'll be the same sort of people advertising in TV as on radio: soap, cornflake and bedtime drink manufacturers. What a pity that publishers cannot for once sink mutual samenesses and get a really impressive show on the air.

Imagine! A gong sounds; a giant book opens slowly and out strides a warrior in leopard skin and glasses. He is shown suddenly in frightening close-up as he says in weighty tones, 'This is the Voice of the Book Trade!'

Gong again. Hans Haas climbs from the Black Sea and begins to write another book before our very eyes. Suave men from Hutchinson's are seen scouring antique shops for material for next year's *Saturday Book*. An old naturalist dashes into Collins' with something struggling wildly inside a fishing net. Explaining all this, the commentator says, 'So we see the great treadwheel of literacy move irrevocably round on its – er, irrevocable round. And now over to the Oxford University Press, where Arnold Toynbee has just had an idea for another book . . .'

TUESDAY

Seems rather odd and empty in shop without Mrs Callow. When Mr B. arrived about ten o'clock this morning, he brought the temporary help with him: Miss Toplady, Miss Adelaide Toplady, a thin and enthusiastic soul of some fifty winters.

Dave and Gudgeon knew her of old. She had to be reintroduced to them and introduced to Peggy Ellis and me, and even to Edith, our dumb office wench.

'I really ought to have come yesterday,' she told me, 'but I was making the Christmas pudding. Still, better late than never: what shall I do first? Dusting? Always essential in a book shop, I know, and never more so than at this time of year.'

For this purpose she has brought her own feather duster and waltzes briskly round the display tables with it. 'Looks like a ruddy fan dance to me,' comments Mr Parsons, passing through the shop to brush down the front. He was not exactly pleased when she claimed his cellar was too dirty and insisted on hanging up her coat in Mr B.'s office.

Given dull job: re-ordering picture postcards. This (involving little responsibility) is meant to be ideal job for me, but find it otherwise. It entails kneeling on lowest part of attic and sorting through seventy different boxes. Thank goodness for half-day!

'All right for you single blokes,' says Mr Parsons, undoing his overall. 'I've got to spend my afternoon distempering the bedroom.'

Been thinking about commercial TV. No good letting publishers handle it: they'd make it too glossy. Antiquarian Booksellers' Association would have to run it – *The Bookshop Show*, featuring people actually coming into a shop and buying books. This might give viewers the idea.

It need not be real shop, fictitious place would possibly be better. It could be modelled on somewhere like Brightfount's, but be smarter of course and situated in more lively area. And with good-looking staff. And intelligent customers.

'Now here is Mrs Thirst of 29 Azalea Crescent just leaving with a copy of *Weft Pirns for Re-winding Cotton and Spun Rayon Yarns for Use in Shuttles* under her arm. Does this book represent any special interest of yours, Mrs Thirst?'

'"Thrust", it is actually, if you don't mind: Mrs Thrust. Well, all my life I've been interested in shuttles, although not so much in shuttles fitted with tongues, for which this book is designed. But the weft pirns is quite a new interest, so to speak.'

'And are you going to buy any other books before you leave here, Mrs Thrust?'

'Oh Lor', no, it's taken them a whole month to get me this one. I'm off after some weft pirns now.'

No, perhaps we'd better leave TV to the bedtime drinks.

Here it is December, and me feeling spring-like! Very nice letter from Sheila, if rather short.

Dear Peter,

I expect you will be wondering why I have not written to you before this, particularly after your sweet letter with all those dear but unmerited things you say about me. I know I should have written before this – but I have just been too busy. My room has no individuality and I have been trying to make it more like me – but alas cannot eradicate a giant structure of mirrors and tiny shelves which stretches from mantelpiece to ceiling. How oddly our ancestors lived, but I wonder if we will seem any better to our descendants.

There are so many orphans at the Adoption Society homes! And although I cannot pretend they are all 'dear little things', they do bring tears to the eyes (I shall either have to grow more hard hearted or have permanent red rings!).

I have thought several times – no, more than that! – of our happy ride to Epley and back. Do you remember our bathe in the summer time, when you stung your foot? That is a long time ago now, isn't it, Peter? And it will be a long time before we meet again – Christmas at the earliest, I suppose. I am really looking forward to that so much – and I will hire a sprig of mistletoe (if that is how you spell it?) especially for the occasion!

Please give my love to Myra and Derek when you see them, and of course to your Uncle and Auntie – and also keep a little for yourself from

Sheila.

PS. – Perhaps I ought to have finished by saying something more special. But I am really a very ordinary sort of girl – and find that sort of thing difficult on paper. Perhaps you will teach me some day.

S.

Very ordinary indeed! Wrote rather subtle letter to Mother, asking her to be sure to ask Sheila over to ours for Christmas.

Back on picture postcards at the shop, but finished them about

4.30. Thoughts had been anywhere but at Brightfount's. Dirty job: had bath early in evening. Mrs Yell's hot tap makes noise like old man grumbling and spitting.

FRIDAY
Pay-day.

After nearly a week of meditation have come to no decision about Aunt and Uncle. Cannot, although I tried even that, avoid the fact that she lied to me, built up, in fact, a whole tissue of lies. Why? Was it something she was doing against me or against Uncle? If only I were better at people's motives.

Feel I must say something on Sunday, get something definite. And if I do, there will probably be horrid bust-up, recriminations, tears, threats of divorce, goodness knows what. Eventually one of them may get locked up as insane: but which, Aunt or Uncle? Or both?

SATURDAY
Rexine still in purgative mood; my turn to get it in the neck. I was rather in panic during afternoon because shop suddenly grew very crowded and Peggy and I were only ones serving downstairs, others had vanished, and several customers claiming attention. As I pushed through crowd towards the till, I heard one man say to another, 'Come on, let's go. What are you looking for now?' To which the other replied morosely, 'I'm looking for a damned assistant.'

'I'm a damned assistant,' I said. 'Is there anything I can get for you?', at which he was properly discomforted. But Rexine, of course, had just appeared at head of cellar stairs and had heard, and said to me in a low, angry voice as he struggled with paper, King Penguins and sellotape, 'After Christmas, we're going to have a tightening up here; I'm going to produce a book of rules for your benefit – yours and Eastwode's.'

'It'll be a classic of the trade,' says Dave grimly when I pass on this titbit. '*Rexine's Complete Guide to Book-Bashing*' – the latter being Dave's familiar name for our calling.

December

This was to be my big scene. But when I got into the act it was already half over, and I had only a walking-on part.

Julie Howells was standing indecisively in Aunt's kitchen, listening to a heated argument going on in the hall. When she saw me, she looked embarrassed to be caught eavesdropping.

'Derek asked me in for a drink,' she whispered. 'It seems to have ignited a fuse of some kind.'

'Have they been at it long?'

'They're just warming up!' She was poised again now. This was a girl, after all, who dealt in ultrasonics.

'I've told you we're going, haven't I, damn it?' Derek's bull-like voice interrupted Aunt's monologue, as I slipped in upon them. Nod ran up barking at me.

'And I don't want to be spoken to like that! To think I should be spoken to like that! By my own son in my own house!' exclaims Aunt in wonder.

'There's more where that came from,' he answered shortly, and in the same breath, 'For heaven's sake, Myra, pull yourself together and help me strap up this bloody, bloody trunk.'

He is bent double in cap and duffle coat, knee on large black cabin trunk, red of face and lugging savagely at leather strap.

148

'Can I help at all?' I ask, by way of infiltration into this tense situation. Whereupon Derek looks up, drops strap, bursts into laughter and exclaims, 'Here we all are, busting up the happy home, and this goon comes in and wants to know if it can help at all!'

He laughs uproariously, and Aunt tells him to control himself. Myra snaps at him to shut up. Aunt turns on me and says, 'Derek and Myra are leaving here. It might be a good idea if you stayed out of the way for a while.'

Asked, 'Where's Uncle Leo? Does he know what he is missing?'

'Your Uncle happens to be over with Colonel Howells. He is well aware what trouble this – this daughter-in-law has been causing' – (furious glance at Myra) – 'although as always he refuses to face facts.'

Aunt very white as she speaks. Myra adds quietly, 'All the same, this little shindy sprang up when he was out.'

Julie is still in background; ask her to go and fetch Uncle, saying, 'A lot seems to go on without his knowing the truth. I want him to *see* what's happening.'

Derek has mastered the trunk and exclaims, 'Don't be a fool, Peter. It's bad enough without Father jawing, too. Myra can't get on with them and that's all there is to it. I could see this coming weeks ago. We'll be all right at Epley – half the house is livable. Now be a good kid and lend me a hand with this confounded coffin.'

Lend him a hand. Julie has gone for Uncle. Aunt begins about filial ingratitude. Myra says it's all her fault and nothing to do with Derek. Derek shouts back over his shoulder that oh yes it is. Tell him that they are all squabbling like children.

He drops trunk at garage door and asks me with studied patience to keep out of it: I don't know all the issues involved. Begin to be annoyed.

'Probably know more than you do,' I tell him. 'Don't forget, I lived with them for four years – you've done little more than see them at week-ends. Why should you clear out like a huffy woman just because there's been an argument? What about your father? Doesn't he deserve a little consideration? Can't you see he's going through an unhappy time?'

'Father's crackers! It makes no difference whether we're here or not!'

'Oh, no? He may behave a little oddly, but he's not so bad as your mother. What about her? You don't know some of the stories she cooks up—'

'Look, if you want a smack in the eye, just say so.'

'I'm sorry, Derek. I'm telling it wrong. What I'm trying to say is that your father and mother want disentangling. It's no good just running away.'

'Oh, isn't it? You want disentangling yourself, Peter. Myra's nearly three months in the family way: she needs taking out of this madhouse – and I include you in that.'

So I am silenced.

Uncle appears from next door, looking worried. Derek starts to explain in the yard, rain comes on and we retire indoors. There the whole argument begins again, although on a saner key.

Root of the matter is that Myra and Aunt, alone together most of the week, dislike each other – or rather, Aunt dislikes Myra. Trouble was touched off this morning because Myra and Derek had been in London yesterday (actually with Sheila!) and came back late after a theatre; after which, Myra asked for breakfast in bed.

Derek says they will be leaving in a month in any event: they might as well leave now.

So Uncle Leo and I are the only ones who want them to stay. I have little say in matter and poor old Uncle's stock has fallen very low since he set light to curtains. He looks very defenceless and humble, and suddenly I blurt out about the D. H. Lawrence story.

Odd sort of silence after this. They all look offended.

'Haven't we got enough troubles without dragging Lawrence of Arabia in?' Derek grumbles in half-hearted fashion. Think at last he begins to see the situation clearly, even if he has his Lawrences muddled.

Hardly dare look at them – but Myra makes silent clapping motion.

Aunt bursts into tears. Uncle goes to her at once.

We clear off and leave them. Derek begins to 'have it out with me', as he calls it. Myra tells him to dry up and think – and suddenly he comes out with brilliant idea: let Aunt go away for a rest.

'The poor girl's tired,' he says. 'She's probably got an unexpurgated copy of *Lady Chatterley's Lover* locked away somewhere and it's gone to her head. We'll ship her off for a week and it'll all blow over.'

So it was settled. Aunt Doris was phoned and said she would love to have her. Aunt Anne agreed with surprising meekness.

Went with some foreboding to make my peace with her before leaving. She looked for a second as if she was not going to speak to me. Then she said, 'No doubt you believe you acted for the best, Peter. You cannot be expected to see into an old lady's mind. My hold on life, you know, is far more tenuous than your uncle's. No – I can see now I was deluded in believeing he has been making attempts against himself. I have been deluded in many ways, my boy. I knew before Derek came home it would bring us no happiness . . .'

'Derek's very fond of you.'

'And I'm very fond of Derek. But he's like your uncle. He needs more control. A man's way in the world is clear cut and easy; a woman's has to be more devious. You understand the longing for a home of your own. I long for a character of my own. I should never have married – oh, you won't comprehend my exact meaning – but to be a wife is to surrender not only your name but your personality.

'Still, I shall be glad to stay with Doris for a time. She *never* had any personality.'

MONDAY
To-day, after a night's sleep, I can grasp yesterday's affair much more clearly. What it boils down to is Uncle Leo's detachment; he has always been self-sufficient. If he wants to do something which requires standing in fish pond, he stands in fish pond. Aunt's dislike of this is understandable: she has to press his trousers.

We had to advertise in *Clique* for *Forever Amber* for someone. Among several quotes which arrived to-day, we were delighted to get one for a copy with 'binding soiled, text sound and clean . . .'

151

Saw Miss Toplady arrive this morning on her new Cyclemaster, a breath-taking spectacle! She lit cigarette as she entered shop, and smoked surreptitiously nearly all day.

She has some difficulty in deciding where to start looking for the books she gets asked for.

'Don't you think this system of arranging them all in sections is rather obsolete?' she inquires of Rexine.

'How would you arrange them?' he asks. Rexine always sounds at his rudest when he puts on that polite tone.

'Why, put them all into one alphabet!' says Miss T.

'With the "A"s in the Attic and the "Z"s in the Slaughterhouse?'

'Er – yes. Or vice versa.'

'And when they come in not knowing the author?'

Pause.

'You don't like my little suggestion, do you, Mr Rexine?'

TUESDAY

Have been in book trade four years to-day. I came in just after Eric Linklater's *Spell for Old Bones* came out. Remember that book particularly because old Mr Parsons and Dave had some joke about it that I never fathomed. Can recall vividly the feeling of terror as my very first customer approached, and Rexine saying afterwards, 'Steady now, remember they are probably as ignorant about books as you are.'

Contrived to remind Mr Brightfount of this historic anniversary during morning, thinking he might like to celebrate the event by giving me a rise, but all he said was, 'Ah, we shall make something of you yet.'

More I think of that remark, less I like it; it was so obviously intended to be encouraging.

Had lunch with Uncle Leo. Aunt went off this morning by train, so he now has his midday meal in town. Myra looks after him at home.

'She's a good girl, Peter. She'll manage Derek well enough. All through history, women have been underestimated, entirely because they cannot herd together as men can. One day, they'll learn that trick, and then – well, I shan't be alive then, thank goodness!'

WEDNESDAY

Half-day.

Seemed to get succession of dreary customers this morning. Sometimes feel like saying to one of them pleadingly, 'My dear madam, you are our only contact with the outside world: please say something!'

Which would probably earn answer like, 'Well, I was just going to ask you if this mark inside the cover was really six shillings. It's a bit expensive for what it is, isn't it? I mean the book was only published at a guinea. I'd take it if it was four and six.'

At such moments, how cheering to turn to the card index of library addresses and see the liberty packed into that small file:

Chipping Campden
Chiswick
Christchurch
Cincinnati

Nothing like a little vicarious travel!

Had pretty quiet afternoon. Mrs Yell came up to my room about six and said, 'Mr Y. and I are going round the corner to Madge's to watch her TV. Wouldn't you like to come with us? I'm sure she wouldn't mind.'

Thought it was very decent of her, went round like a shot. Chief offering of the evening was long excerpt from Gounod's *Faust*, which we all watched without a word.

'Smashing!' declared Mrs Yell's sister afterwards. 'I'm getting a proper opera fan! The only thing I couldn't understand was why he fell out with that Mestoph – oh, you know, that handsome, dark gentleman.'

THURSDAY

Mrs Callow still away with bad leg. 'I am prepared to stay as long as I can be of any assistance,' declares Miss Toplady magnanimously, and we begin to fear she may become a permanency. She's quite amusing in her way, but inclined to preach, also she has taken unreasoning dislike to poor old Gudgeon, who is quite harmless; perhaps it is the curious way he looks at her.

'I have a feeling he is not sympathetic to books,' she is reported to have remarked to Arch Rexine. To which Rexine caustically replied, 'He's only here to sell 'em, not baby-sit for them, you know.'

So she has now taken a reasoning dislike to Rexine. We feel Rexine went a bit too far – not, as Dave remarked, that we expected him to go an inch less.

Rather charming to see how Peggy has taken Miss T. under her wing. Perhaps she is glad to have someone about who knows even less than herself.

Wrote long letter to Sheila, chiefly telling her about the 'do' on Sunday.

FRIDAY
Pay-day. Perishing cold.

SATURDAY
Woke to find a pepper-and-salting of snow everywhere. White Christmas coming up?

Charming letter from new American customer, who orders several books and adds, 'As I have done no business with you before, gentlemen, I will mention as a reference that for years I have been a regular subscriber to *Punch*.'

Sold two picture postcards of Bagger's Lane with gasometers in background during morning, and that was about all. Afternoon hectic, however. Christmas cards going steadily.

Staggered back to digs to find Mr Yell dolefully tacking up streamers in hall. 'Watch out for the missus,' he warned. 'She's in a fearful temper. Take my tip – if your kipper's a bit overdone, just keep your mouth shut! Oh, and hand us up that big bell, will you?'

Over tea, I got the facts of the case from Mrs Y. 'Someone who shall be nameless' had left 'his dog' in the kitchen without due surveill-ance, and only a broken plate and a few crumbs remained where a freshly baked Christmas cake had been before. '*His* dog' was now locked out for the evening: poor old Gyp always belongs to Mr Y. when he's in trouble.

Shop fairly full most of week. Despite commercial efforts to begin Christmas trade earlier each year, many people prefer to leave things nearer the time. Perhaps it is laziness, perhaps a pleasant sense of spending in genial Christmas mood. Somehow the snow does lend a festive touch. The nearer the Great Day, the intenser the enjoyment of buying all these smart, bright things. Half this pleasure is doubtless relief: that's Aunt Veronica settled!

As a lady bought a gardening book off me this afternoon, she said, 'It looks horribly dull to me, but I've never managed to give him anything he's liked yet.'

Must be wretched to give presents to people like that! I am going to give Mrs Yell a bottle of bath salts, and I know she'll be as over-whelmed as if they were the Crown Jewels.

Amazing how many people still buy books! Despite wet and cold, they tramp in and look busily round the shelves, buying quite a bit. To-day we actually sold a shabby, worm-eaten set of *Oceans and Oceans of Story* (which has lain at the top of the stairs for years to my knowledge) to nautical-looking bod; wonder if he was expecting nautical stories?

The sea, under or on top, is much in vogue. *The Captain's Table*, *The Blue Continent*, or old stagers like *Kon-Tiki* and *Cruel Sea*, all go steadily, as does *The Multitudinous Seas*, in its smart incarnadine jacket. Latter is apparently so realistic publishers give away life-jacket with every copy.

SUNDAY
Gyp was sick in his kennel last night.

'That's the Lord teaching you not to be greedy!' Mrs Yell admonishes him.

'It don't say much for the cake, either,' adds Mr Yell.

More snow everywhere – quite a bit still falling as I cycled cautiously out to 'Hatchways'. Was interested to see how things were going there with Aunt away, but everything much the same. Very cheerful lunch.

'It's a good job Myra and I didn't clear off last week,' Derek observes from a full mouth. 'It's as damp as the bottom of a well over at Epley. We've got fires going now – I've got the electricity back on.'

'Speaking of electricity,' says Uncle Leo, 'that reminds me. While your Mother's away I'm going to have a little surprise for her. The upper landing light can be switched off from upstairs or down, but the only switch for the hall light is in the hall. We always leave it on when going up to bed, which means an unnecessary journey back again to put it off.

'I'm going to get a man to fix up a switch for us so that the hall light will go off from the bedroom. Anne should like that.'

Derek looks at him suspiciously.

'I should give that sort of stunt a miss for a bit,' he says.

Now back in digs, which are cold and uninviting, despite a saucer with two mince pies standing on my table, beside which is a note:
HOPE YOU HAD NICE DAY. GONE TO SEE MADGE'S TV. VERA YELL.

She's a dear old soul, Mrs Yell, but I wish her blessed gasfire worked properly.

To bed early.

MONDAY
Boris Maclaren in – a poor start to anyone's week. Generally he will only speak to Rexine or Mr B., but they were upstairs in Mr B.'s room chewing over 'the figures', or something equally mysterious; only Dave, Miss Toplady and I were about, and we obviously didn't look very promising.

Dave, knowing Maclaren, said to Miss Toplady who didn't, 'You serve that bloke; I'm just going down to the cellar.'

She innocently inquired of this famous boor, who once filled four pages of *Picture Post*, if there was anything he wanted. He ceased snuffling among the old bindings and fixed her with a bilious eye.

'I'm seeking a brief address entitled *An Admonition to the Parliament* for a fellow scholar,' he said severely. 'It was published in

1572, and inspired a reply from Richard Hooker – ah, I don't think it remotely likely you will have it.'

'Oh, I'm sure we haven't!' said Miss T. brightly. 'But if your friend is religious, wouldn't he like a copy of *The Robe*?'

It might have been my imagination, but I thought Brightfounts' foundations shuddered. Maclaren certainly did. He stared transfixed at her inanely innocent face and then said, 'Psssmrrgh! You – you product of your environment, madam!' and then stomped out of the shop.

Decided to go out for a long walk after tea. Air was glorious, sky so clear that stars hardly twinkled. On the town roads snow has been churned into mashed potato and gravy, but along Upper Wickham road, where it has been allowed to settle, it looks like white marble.

And to think – it's Christmas next week!

TUESDAY

Breakfast burnt again! I know man cannot live by bread alone, but would almost prefer it to Mrs Yell's toast.

Good few people about, despite cold; it's certainly warm in Brightfount's. Mr B. has his cough again. He received a terse letter from Boris M. this morning: we didn't think *he* would let slip opportunity to make trouble. It complained of 'incompetents masquerading as know-alls' and suggested such people should not be allowed to serve in shop.

This puts Mr B. on spot, Miss Toplady being a friend of the family. We hope Mrs Callow will be back next week; meanwhile her stand-in has been tactfully requested to go upstairs and help Gudgeon on forthcoming Topography catalogue. To this Miss Toplady has agreed, not from any love of Gudgeon, but because it allows her to smoke – which she does plentifully at every opportunity!

Returned home in evening to find letter awaiting me beside my plate.

'Don't recognize that handwriting,' remarks Mrs Yell frankly.

Tell her, 'I hardly do myself!'

It is from Andrew, who begins in ingratiating fashion:

My Dear Little Brother,

Doubtless you will read this with your eye in a fine frenzy rolling, wondering what on earth might tempt or prompt me to write to you. The pupil will soon learn.

Mother tells me that your letters home recently have mentioned with somewhat suspicious frequency the female christian name Sheila. Whether we are to attach more importance to this than to the earlier but similarly enthusiastic repetitions of the words Maureen, Judy, Jean – were there not *two* Jeans about here? – Helen, Avril and Mary (I trust I have them in correct sequence), I know not.

But if we *are* to, may I interpose a word of brotherly cheer and say, 'Go to, son!' If this girl, woman, sibyl, has merit, seize her while she's on the market. Take, in short, the plunge.

These things must be done while the fire's i' the blood, before you reach an age of discretion. A few more years shall roll and, without wishing in the least to spread gloom around, you will then be of my sager years: in a word, thirty-one.

And then it will be too late. You will no longer be armed with your splendid trust in women. It is sad but it is so. Marry her now!

However. Not to commit this pearl to paper did I write. There is a baser object . . . to remind you in your provincial retreat that Christmas draws nigh, the season of festivity, goodwill and present-giving. It is in connection with the latter that I particularly wish to speak.

Will you kindly see to it that I receive either a really good watch, an elaborate piece of photographic equipment or a bone-buttoned waistcoat of archaic design? Or, if your wretched stipend will not run to these, a copy of Cecil Beaton's *Glass of Fashion*.

> Thine only brother,
> from whom all blessings,
> Andrew.

Odd the way Andrew writes, since he talks nothing like that. Odd, too, that although the concepts 'marriage' and 'Sheila' have often been in my mind, it should be he who first connects them together.

WEDNESDAY

Rush on, to-day being early closing. Traveller in to see Mr B. so Dave and I hard-pressed. Both savage with Gudgeon, who had some cataloguing to do in front room upstairs and sat avoiding customers' eyes.

Fortunately Rexine caught him staring absently out of window, picking his teeth on corner of index card, and had him downstairs in the mêlée. Miss Toplady had popped out at the time to get 'one weenie little Christmas present'.

Amazing: sold three copies of *Folk Tunes of These Isles* during morning. Singing fifteen bob in the till each time and a bow bow bow in the sweet derry bush.

Poor old Gaspin came in, would ramble on in his usual vein while we were trying to serve. 'Oh, it's nice to see the people in,' he said, smiling benignly at an old soul for whom I was wrapping a Phaidon. 'After all, don't you know, a bookshop is the true meeting point of ivory tower and market place.' As the old soul pushed smartly past him on the way to the door, he added, '. . . something too much of the market place,' and left.

THURSDAY

Met my charming Lady Mary on way back to digs yest. afternoon. Said she: 'You've been avoiding me!' Not true, despite her expensive tastes and her R.A.F. friend. But somehow the urge was gone. Was as nice as possible, chatted about the thaw and left her. No doubt about it, a big change is coming over me.

Snow nearly gone, apart from few dirty patches in Arraway's garden and such wildernesses.

This is time of year when booksellers really begin to worry. It is now too late to expect to get anything you order from publishers before Christmas. Stock, however, going rapidly, Christmas cards likewise. Spent evening doing my cards.

Funny how books on how to be an author sell, even in nonliterary area like this. Suppose everyone is politician or author at heart.

Working in bookshop gives you pretty good idea of world of literature. Yet it is easy to forget that after all we float on only the exposed seventh part of great iceberg of literacy (which, to get the metaphor really between my teeth, has broken off the glacier of cogitation and is now at large in the ocean of world affairs, a menace in the shipping lanes of ignorance) – where was I? Oh, yes, only one unsolicited manuscript in two thousand ever slips into print. So that although about twelve or thirteen thousand new books (far more than anyone can cope with!) appear in a year, the number that don't appear is much more impressive.

And oppressive! Think of all that vast, subterranean labour, all the headaches in back rooms, all gone for nothing. No, not for nothing; the man or woman who, untutored, has had the staying power to write an eighty thousand word novel is entitled to respect, whether it has appeared in 12 point Bembo solid or remains Biro in exercise book.

FRIDAY

Pay-day. Bought Beaton's *Glass of Fashion* for Andrew: he deserves it! Family mostly get books for presents – near relations new ones, distant relations remainders.

Dave in trouble again. He arrived late, crept in the side door and called to Peggy in stage whisper, 'Has any wreck seen Rexine?' a joke we hear at least once a week from Dave.

Whereupon Rexine appeared from stationery bay and said, 'If you're looking for me to ask me the time, it's gone ten past nine.'

Thus crushed, Dave helped me re-do the window, which was considerably plundered yesterday. We piled about everything in there we could find. We've got a remainder called *The Parson in English Literature* by a man named Christmas, and Dave stuck this in the middle with a notice saying '5s. only. By Christmas – for Christmas'. I thought this was rather good, but when Mr B. arrived he spotted

161

it and said, 'That sort of thing's all very well for Pardon's but it's too smart Alick for us.' So out the notice came.

Fall of snow again.

'Here,' Dave said during afternoon. 'When you get a chance, pop upstairs and just go quietly into the Topog. room. Only don't say I sent you.'

Got a chance later on, when looking out a couple of books we reported months ago to a man in Dundee. Old Gudgeon and Miss Toplady were sitting together at the table, Gudgeon smoking one of her cigarettes and showing her how to type a catalogue slip. A perfect picture! – Marred only by Gudgeon looking up and saying pettishly, 'Hurry up and close the door, will you? There's a draught round my – Miss Toplady's ankles – er, feet.'

Went back downstairs with a wild surmise in my heart!

Brief note from Aunt Anne. Could have been worse.

She said she was much enjoying rest, had less to worry her than at Folkestone (whatever that meant), she was looking forward to seeing me again on Sunday, hoped I would come up as usual, Auntie Doris sent her love, and she was my ever forgiving Auntie Anne!

SATURDAY

Heyday! People really making up minds to spend. Mr B. helping in shop, as was even Gudgeon, some of the time.

Christmas is one time of year when people will buy more or less what is in stock. How cheering to see some of the stickers being wrapped up and carried off! Often decisive factor is not contents but state of jacket. Must be ghastly to be publisher just now, sitting back with fingers crossed, helpless. At least we're at the customer's elbow to say, 'I remember *The Sunday Times* gave it a good review when it came out.'

As Edith was emptying tills and Dave and I putting our coats on, Gudgeon was seen nipping upstairs.

'Not going home to-night?' Dave asked.

'Er – not just yet,' Grudgeon said. 'Bit behindhand with that catalogue. Got to be at Jukes' by February.'

'Miss Toplady still up there?'

'Well . . . yes, she has kindly consented to stay and help me,' he said. 'Just for – hey!'

But Dave took no notice of his shout, and continued whistling Wagner's 'Wedding March' as he went out into the night.

SUNDAY

All fine at 'Hatchways', except Nod; the Howells' cat scratched his nose last week.

The whole lot of them – *and* Sheila! – are coming over to ours for Christmas. Only Uncle and Aunt will sleep at ours, the others will put up at 'The Box and Cox'. Uncle will drive Aunt and Myra over on Friday morning, Derek will drive Sheila up from London.

Left early, as had a date at Mrs Callow's. Old Dave was also there. She is now out of plaster and in fine spirits. House very decorative and Christmassy. Carol singers called just after I arrived.

We had plenty to eat, and then played several games, mostly of her devising – including one of her brain-splitting literary ones. Object was for us each to make cryptic representation of a book title. Mr Callow did charming drawing of a Provençal beauty, all eyelashes; Dave guessed this, marvellous to relate – 'The French Eyes are Fair' (*The Franchise Affair*). But Mrs Callow's really stumped us all: it was nothing but a long, thin capital 'A'. Even after her hint that it represented a Mark Twain title, we did not get it. When she finally explained it was 'In No Sense "A" Broad' (*Innocents Abroad*), we disqualified her unanimously for thinking it up beforehand.

PS. – New Year's Resolution: when customers ask for book not in stock, I resolve not to say, 'I'm so sorry, we had a copy, but it was sold yesterday.' It may be almost irresistible, but it's not consoling!

MONDAY

Christmas week.

Sneaked in side door bit late, but in time to hear familiar voice talking to Dave.

'Hello, Mrs Callow,' I said, 'how does it feel to be back?'

'Splendid, thanks. The hospital is sending my leg on later.'

'Rexine missed you no end,' Dave said. 'We've hardly had a decent word out of him . . . Gudgeon won't be pleased to see you, though.' And he told her about G. and Miss Toplady, with suitable embellishments. Then a customer came in for an exercise book and we dispersed.

When Gudgeon appeared, however, he did seem genuinely pleased to see her, in his odd way, and asked solicitously after her leg.

'It's on a much firmer footing now, thank you,' she said. 'But I'm sorry to hear about your conduct while I've been away.'

'I don't like the way you say that. You mean – misconduct?'

'I mean Miss Toplady. Dave tells me you two have been getting off.'

Gudgeon mutters something about telling Dave where he gets off, and disappears upstairs. The lady in question arrived on her Cyclemaster about ten, looked rather freezingly at Mrs Callow and said that as she was here now she might as well stay. Lighting a cigarette, she retired upstairs.

At lunch time she said good-bye to us all very graciously. Think she quite enjoyed her stay here. All rather touched to see a little chromium ashtray Gudgeon gave her as a parting gift.

TUESDAY

Uncle Leo sheepishly appeared in shop, nodded to me, saying, 'Taking the morning off – nobody gives each other parcels of land for Christmas,' and went upstairs to see Mr B. He was down again in few moments; I was not serving, and asked him what he was doing.

He squared his shoulders, making himself as big as possible. 'I've just arranged to buy up Brightfount's,' he said brightly. 'It's all settled.'

At the look of disconsolence which passed over my face, his whole attitude changed. He shook his head and said gravely, 'I'm sorry, Peter, I'm only trying to be funny. I just came in to wish old Bernard a Happy Christmas. Your Aunt's going to collect me in a moment: she wishes to give me a new overcoat for a present, and so we are about to proceed to Dungfloss's to see what he has on his hangers.'

And as Aunt appeared he added hastily, 'Don't look so worried – it's Christmas!'

They took me to the Odalisque for lunch. All seemed well between them. Myra and Derek move into their house on New Year's Day, and think Aunt will be happier then, as she seems to have knife into Myra.

It makes New Year sound close! Brightfount's shuts for one day and a notice on the door says, 'These premises are closed for stock-taking for one day only.'

Behind the notice, we all engage feverishly on taking down every book and adding up their prices, shelf by weary shelf. Before the notice, those who cannot read rattle vainly on the door without effect. Funny how many illiterates require a bookshop when it's shut; open, we have a job attracting the literates.

Our dumb office wench, Edith, was star turn of last stocktaking. Arriving in horrible frame of mind after late night and too much British sherry, she was dressed in tight blue jeans with head-square round skull. Jeans and head-squares do little for any girl: for Edith they are positively ruinous. She refused to speak to anyone, descended into cellar and took stock of all filthiest sets she could find, raising as much dust as possible.

Even Arch Rexine could not have induced her down there when she was in good temper.

Miss Harpe was with us then. She was almost useless at stocktaking. Not only was dust anathema to her, she had no head for figures or heights and so could not add up or climb a ladder.

WEDNESDAY
Marvellous letter from Sheila. It does really sound as if she likes me. Shall have to do something, somehow, about earning more money in New Year.

Weather warm and muggy of a sudden, as if it wants to be unobtrusive as poss. For travellers at week-end. Everyone in good spirits, except Mr Parsons, who disappeared into his cellar muttering something about 'mild Christmas, full graveyard'.

Shop crowded all morning. Christmas cards very low, but still being picked over. This is the 'last moment' period, when worried little men rush in and select something at random for forgotten nieces – what Mrs Callow calls 'running around in Thirkells'.

And to think: next Wednesday we shall be busy sorting away the debris and it will all be over! We shall clear up the clutter and fold away the pretty paper, remove Christmas cards from window and stow away less conspicuously the numberless pencil sharpeners disguised as tricycles, dog kennels, space-ships and violins, etc.

Sometimes it staggers me to think that books manage to retain their conservative shape. World of commerce, like the insect world, is full of things camouflaged as something else: hotwater bottles like scotties, perfume like ships, nutcrackers like crocodiles, soap like Popeye. How easy it would be to bring out the next George Sava shaped like a medicine bottle, how fatally easy to think of appropriate shapes for books issued by publishers like Bell or Chambers.

It would certainly be a help when customers came in for a book whose title they had forgotten to be able to ask, 'Well, can you tell me what it looked like?'

'Oh, yes, it was shaped like a 1950 Daimler' – or, 'It was about the size and shape of a sewing machine' – or, 'The copy I saw could be used as a salad bowl once you had read it.'

Still, they don't remember author, title, publisher or subject: don't suppose they'd be any more likely to remember shape.

Christmas letter with four handkerchiefs from Aunt Doris awaiting me when I got back to Mrs Yell's. She finished by saying, 'Aunt tells me that you are attracted to Myra's sister – Sonia, is it? I forget. You won't mind my saying I know, as an auntie of long standing, that we shall all be glad if you settle down. But although I have no silly prejudices I was sorry when Anne told me that the sisters are half-castes. Is it Sonia or Sheila now I think of it?'

So Aunt Anne has evidently lost none of her inventive verve!

THURSDAY
Had to take something round to the library. Ruth smiled brightly, made indications of being friendly. Said 'Merry Christmas' in as surly fashion as I dare.

Came back via High Street. Pardon's very busy when I passed it. Could see Reggie inside looking so harassed that I almost went in to help him. (Wonder what would happen if people like he and Rexine suddenly lost faith?!). Interesting to see how other trades cash in on this season. The arty-crafty shop next door to Pardon's displays a large banner saying 'A Festive Board Needs Bodger's Candles', while Weevle, the ironmonger's, flaunts the lying message 'It isn't Christmas without a Tay-Stee-Toaster'; even the Bottomley Place chemists, Loghead and Beale, advise 'Win her with Yoga's "Pride" this Xmas-tide', an unexpectedly romantic hint from such a staid old firm.

How uncommercial the book trade is! We don't have slogans; the books can speak for themselves. Which is a pity in a way – it means we miss a lot of gems. Even existing national sales-lines could be twisted into publishing use. What about

Good evenings begin with Gollancz, or
Have you Macmillanned your mind to-day? or
Seckervescence lasts the whole book through.

FRIDAY
Christmas Eve! Ah, that magical feeling of excitement again, fresh each year. It's the 6.50 train home for me to-night, and then no more work till next Wednesday: four days with Sheila in the offing. If I don't say something irrevocable to her, so help me!

Writing this before breakfast. Got up early to pack. Mr Y. went to work whistling a carol: otherwise it might be just an ordinary day so far. It just does not *feel* ordinary.

Later: Tucked up in bed at home.

Think that from this Christmas at Brightfount's two incidents will remain in my mind, one sad, one funny. Shop was almost deserted this morning when an old lady came in with a schoolboy. They looked rather forlornly round shelves, and finally I asked if I could help at all, whereupon woman said, 'We're looking for something second-hand for Dad's Christmas present that won't be too expensive.' Spent long time hunting for them, at last found *Complete Home Carpentering* for 3s. 6d., with which they were overjoyed. Do hope Dad liked it, too.

Then, earlier in the week, when Rexine and I were holding the fort alone during lunch hour, in absolute throng of people, an old girl in a fur grabbed me by arm and said, 'Could you find me a Christmas card suitable for one little pussy to send another little pussy?'

Quiet in afternoon, although one or two desperate folk in. Amazing how soon they'll lose that bright acquisitive look!

Upstairs, Gudgeon, Mrs Callow and Mr B. were winding up the catalogue. Dave and I, feeling we'd done well and needed rest, chatted over the counter. Apparently Edith has mistletoe and chestnuts up in the Attic; she invited Dave up there, but he would not try the one for fear of the other.

And then in came Miss Toplady! She was smoking and bore a bottle of South African sherry; with this she disappeared downstairs and made her peace with Mr Parsons. One at a time we joined them down there, going cautiously past Rexine's office. Gudgeon was prised quietly away from Mr B.

At 5.30 we finally closed and banged up shutters and blinds. By then Gudgeon had left to catch an early train to Winchelsea. Mr Brightfount and Arch Rexine were presented, as usual, with cigars and Dry Sack respectively. Whereupon we all descended for a final sip of Miss Toplady's sherry before making off.

Dave and I left together by the side door, followed by Rexine's cheerful 'Merry Christmas! – And don't be late next Wednesday morning!'

Printed by RR Donnelley at Glasgow, UK